The Night Spies

by

Kathy Kacer

Second
Story
Press

NATIONAL LIBRARY OF CANADA CATALOGUING IN PUBLICATION DATA

Kacer, Kathy, 1954-
The night spies / Kathy Kacer.

(The Holocaust remembrance series for young readers)
ISBN 978-1-896764-70-2

1. World War, 1939-1945--Underground movements--Czechoslovakia--
Juvenile fiction. 2. World War, 1939-1945--Children--Czechoslovakia--
Juvenile fiction.
I. Title. II. Series: Holocaust remembrance book for young readers.

PS8571.A33N53 2003   jC813'.54   C2003-900552-6
                        PZ7

Edited by Sarah Silberstein Swartz
Cover art by Petra Bockus
Designed by Laura McCurdy

Photos on pages 190 and 192 reproduced with the kind permission of
Yad Vashem Archive.

Printed and bound in Canada

*Second Story Press gratefully acknowledges the support of the Ontario Arts
Council and the Canada Council for the Arts for our publishing program. We
acknowledge the financial support of the Government of Canada through the
Book Publishing Industry Development Program, and the Government of
Ontario through the Ontario Media Development Corporation's
Ontario Book Initiative.*

Published by
SECOND STORY PRESS
20 Maud Street, Suite 401
Toronto, Ontario, Canada
M5V 2M5

www.secondstorypress.ca

DEDICATION

In memory of my late grandmother, Marishka Korach Offenberg — a woman of great dignity and courage.

For my children, Gabi and Jake.

ACKNOWLEDGEMENTS

A FEW YEARS AGO, Margie Wolfe of Second Story Press took a chance on an unknown author. I am forever indebted and grateful to Margie for her encouragement and her ongoing enthusiasm. She launched my writing career and has continued to support it.

Thanks also to Laura McCurdy and Carolyn Foster of Second Story Press for their creative contributions to this project.

I cannot begin to express my gratitude to Sarah Swartz — editor extraordinaire — who was determined to help make this the best book possible. I am a better writer today, due in large part to Sarah's wisdom and guidance.

I have a wonderful circle of family members. Thanks to all the Epsteins, Dennills, Kagans and Adlers for listening to my stories, attending my readings, feeding me on Friday nights and providing me with your love. I return it ten-fold.

My husband, Ian Epstein, and my children, Gabi and Jake, are a driving force in my life. They keep me grounded, make me laugh, and challenge and inspire me every day. I love them madly and I am grateful for their confidence in my writing.

Prologue

October 1944

IN THE FIELD

"HALT!" A soldier's voice bellowed from the distance. "Stand still and don't move."

Terrified, Gabi came to an abrupt stop on the hillside, as a dozen Nazi soldiers surrounded them. The Nazis pointed their pistols at the children — Gabi, Max, and Eva. Their bodies cast giant shadows from the sunlight that was just rising over the mountains behind them, filtering through the thick forest beyond the hillside field. Here in the open pasture, neither the cover of the forest nor the safety of their hiding place in the mountain village could protect the children. Instead, they stood out conspicuously, moving amongst the herd of cows.

Gabi felt her breathing become rapid and shallow. Her legs felt weak and, for a moment, she was afraid she might fall. She ran a shaky hand through her blond, curly hair and then shoved her trembling arms into the pockets of her worn overalls. Desperately, she commanded her body to relax.

Max stood frozen next to his older cousin Gabi. Though he always tried to show that he was brave, right now he felt terrified. His brown eyes behind his glasses were round and bulging, as the sinister looking commander of the Nazi patrol towered over them.

In the distance, the mountains rose majestically, dwarfing everything else with their grandeur. Below, tiny farmhouses and barns dotted the landscape. From the field, through the early morning shadows, Gabi could see the barn — their hiding place — and anxiously thought of Mama. Was Mama watching from behind a slit in the walls of the barn? Would she see the soldiers surrounding the children on the hill? She would be desperate to protect them, but helpless to do anything. As for Gabi, as much as she had hated being forced to live inside the barn, for once that was exactly where she longed to be — safe in the hayloft with Max, next to her mother. Curled up in the hay together, she often dreamed about the end of the war and the day they could return home. But at this moment, Mama seemed as unreachable as their real home and freedom.

"What is your name?" the tall Nazi officer barked, as he stared down at Gabi.

Gabi opened and closed her mouth. Frantically she turned to look over at Mr. Kos, who had stopped guiding the cows down the hill, once the Nazi patrol caught up with them. If it weren't for Mr. Kos and his wife, Gabi and her family would have been deported to the concentration camps by now. At a time when so many people were prepared to turn in their Jewish neighbors, Mr. Kos had proven himself a righteous person, risking his life to help Gabi and her family. If the Nazis were to discover that Mr. Kos, a Christian farmer, was helping a Jewish family, he could be arrested or even killed.

How will we get out of this predicament this time, Gabi wondered. Gabi had been only eight years old in 1939 when this horrible war had started. Young though she was, as a Jewish child she had already lived through many difficult experiences. Now she was fourteen and the end of the war and the defeat of Adolf Hitler and his evil Nazis finally seemed near. Had she and her family come this far, only to have everything taken away now?

Next to Mr. Kos stood his granddaughter Eva. As the Nazi officer continued to shout orders, Eva took a step closer to her grandfather. She reached over to place her hand in the safety of his. In her usually sparkling blue eyes was a look of fear. When the Nazi soldiers had started chasing them in the forest, Eva had done the only thing she could think of. She knew these woods well and had led Gabi and Max to her grandfather who was out at dawn, bringing his cows to the hillside field to graze. Her grandfather would protect them, she had thought. He would not let the Nazis harm the children.

Mr. Kos moved protectively in front of the children. Despite his advanced age, Stephan Kos stood up straight, confronting the officer. He was a small but powerful man, his body toughened from years of farm labor. "Is there a problem, sir?" he asked the soldier, speaking strongly but respectfully. "I have done nothing wrong. I am a poor farmer, tending my herd. My cows are restless and I'm trying to bring them back to the barn. And these are my grandchildren, sir. They've come to help me with my herd." The lie quickly rolled off Mr. Kos's tongue. "It's so difficult to find help these days. So many of the young men have been drafted into the armies, as I'm sure you know."

The officer's eyes narrowed as he looked back at Mr. Kos. "Am I talking to you? I'm speaking to the girl. Let her talk." Once again, he turned to face Gabi. "I asked you a question. What is your name?"

It seemed to Gabi that everything depended on how she would respond to him — her own safety, as well as the lives of Max, Mama, Eva, and Mr. and Mrs. Kos. She needed to speak calmly and confidently. She would need to convince the soldiers that she was a local farm girl or she would give them all away. Gabi knew she had been brave in the past. Now she must steady herself and think carefully about what she would say to the officer.

Drumming up her courage, Gabi took a deep breath and briefly closed her eyes. For a second, she tried to block out from her mind their hiding place, the raid in the forest that had just occurred, and the Nazi soldier facing her now. The world faded as Gabi felt herself transported back in time. She remembered the winter morning, less than one year earlier, when Joseph's truck had arrived at the church in this village, carrying its three frightened passengers.

Chapter One

January 1944

EARLY ARRIVAL

IT WAS JUST BEFORE six o'clock in the morning when Joseph's truck pulled into the village of Olsavica in the northern part of Czechoslovakia, the country where Gabi lived. The trip had been long, almost four hours, but gratefully uneventful. Mama and Max had even managed to fall asleep, lulled by the rhythm of the truck winding its way up the mountain road. Each time Gabi had tried to close her eyes, her sleep had been filled with nightmares of being captured by the Nazis. In the end, she decided it was better to stay awake.

But still the dark visions did not disappear. These were terrifying times for thirteen-year-old Gabi and her eleven-year-old cousin Max. They and Gabi's mother were running for their lives, escaping to the mountains to hide from the Nazis. The raids on Gabi's hometown had intensified as the Nazis searched for any remaining Jews. Gabi's house was no longer a safe place. She prayed that in this mountain village, where no one knew them, her family would be well protected and safe.

During the drive, Gabi could not block out the images of what was happening in Europe, especially to Jewish families. Since 1939, when Germany had invaded Poland and started this war, people everywhere seemed to hate Jews. But long before that, the Nazis had introduced tight laws and rules about where Jewish people could go, whom they could have as their friends, what they could own, and where they had to live. By 1940, Jewish families were losing their homes and their businesses. In 1942, Gabi and other Jewish children were no longer allowed to go to school.

Life became most frightening when Jewish families were arrested and sent to "work" at terrible prisons called concentration camps, where Jewish men, women, and children were starved, tortured, and killed. At first, there were only rumors that these places were killing grounds, talk that no one believed. But recently, the rumors were becoming more convincing. People, especially Jews, were terrified of being sent to the camps. Gabi and her mother kept hoping that things would get better and that the war would soon end. But things only seemed to get worse. They worried that they too would soon be sent away. By the time Max arrived at their home in January 1944, Mama and Gabi's plans to leave their home and go into hiding were already in place.

Joseph shifted the gears of his truck, cranking the motor loudly, as he glanced into his rear view mirror at his three passengers. He caught Gabi's eye and smiled reassuringly at her. Joseph had lived next to Gabi's family since before she was born. A few months earlier, he had helped another Jewish family escape by arranging safe passage for them on a train to Switzerland. Joseph never really talked about it, but Gabi's mother knew he was part of the Czech resistance, a secret group that tried to help Jews hide or escape and supplied them with food and clothing in these difficult times. When Gabi and her family knew they were in trouble, he was the obvious person to approach. The danger to Joseph for offering assistance to a Jewish family was enormous. But he had agreed to help them without question. In spite of the risks, there were still some people, like Joseph, who were committed to helping Jews. They didn't use guns to resist the Nazis, but they were very effective. If only more people were like that, thought Gabi, maybe this war would not be happening.

Gabi shuddered and shifted again in her seat inside the truck, careful not to awaken Mama. Joseph's vehicle offered little protection from the freezing winter air. Gabi watched her icy breath trail up and disappear into wisps of smoke. She reached over to wipe the frost from the window, glancing up at the familiar mountains that dominated this part of Czechoslovakia. The mountains were commanding in any season. But in winter, they looked most magnificent, their snowcapped peaks framed against the clear blue sky, like a landscape painting. Despite the early hour and the cold, the cows were already out, moving lazily on the hills above the village. Beyond the hills, the village was surrounded by forest — a jungle of thick, densely packed trees and bush. Gabi could see a narrow path trailing up behind the farmhouses and disappearing into the woods. She shuddered, thinking how terrifying it would be to get lost in those woods.

Papa used to take us up here to these mountains for holidays, recalled Gabi sadly. What would he say about this trip? Gabi could not believe that more than two years had passed since Papa's death. In that time, life had become so much harder for Gabi and her mother. She missed Papa's strength, his wisdom, and his caring presence.

Joseph's truck lurched over the unpaved, rough main road of the village, sending its passengers swaying back and forth. Joseph swerved to avoid hitting the chickens and geese that roamed freely on the road. Small, modest farmhouses lined the road on either side, each one of identical white stone and red, white, and yellow painted wood. Every house had a small plot of land to the side and a small barn in the back.

Picturesque though it was, this was a tiny farming village with poor people and crude homes, nothing like the fine old stone house that Gabi and her family had left behind. Gabi's family had owned many acres of land on which they grew wheat, oats, barley, and potatoes and raised animals. She closed her eyes, wishing she could return to that home but knowing that this was no longer possible. At least we will be safe in one of these houses, she thought, with a family that is willing to hide us.

Up ahead, Gabi could see the stone church that was at the center of the town. And just behind it stood the town hall. Approaching the village, the church was the first thing one noticed — a majestic stone building, crowned with a black tiled roof. The church was modest in size, but its impressive steeple dominated the village, protectively looking out over its congregation of farmers and their families. Joseph's truck headed in that direction and pulled to a stop behind the church tower.

Mama stirred, opened her eyes, and blinked several times, while Max stretched and yawned, adjusting his glasses. His cap was pulled low over his dark, curly hair, but it couldn't hide the permanent fear in his eyes. Gabi thought back a month earlier, to the day Max had arrived at her home, late at night and all alone.

"The Nazis took my mother and father. And they took Julia too," he had declared solemnly, as soon as Mama let him in. His skinny body shivered violently in the winter night's air, his face pale as chalk.

"Max, darling, how did you ever get here?" Mama questioned him anxiously, peering into the darkness to see if anyone else was there. These days when someone banged on the door at night, it usually meant trouble: soldiers coming to arrest you or bad news about a relative or friend.

Max had walked alone from his town in eastern Czechoslovakia to his aunt's home. It was a dangerous journey of more than ten kilometers through the forest between his home and theirs, over several large hills and across roads that were patrolled by soldiers. Nazi soldiers were constantly in search of a wayward Jew whom they might hurt for their own amusement. It was a miracle that Max had made it to their house safely.

"The soldiers took my mother and father. They took everyone," he repeated, trying to stifle the tears that spilled out under his glasses. "I was out trying to find some food and when I got back, Mama, Papa, and Julia had disappeared. The house was a mess and they were gone. Mrs. Landa from next door told me the soldiers had come while I was out. They banged on the door and when no one answered, they broke the door down, went in, and forced everyone outside and onto their truck. Mrs. Landa said it happened in a minute and then they were gone. And then she added that I had better leave or the soldiers would come back for me. She said, 'These days, one less Jew means one less headache.' I didn't know what else to do, so I came here."

"Oh no!" screamed Mama. "Not my brother — not our family too." She struggled to gain control over herself and hugged Max, trying to calm his slight, trembling body as her own mind tried to cope with the news of her brother's arrest. "You must have been terrified, my poor boy." Mama swallowed hard and clutched her nephew to her chest. "Tell me again, Max," she asked more gently. "Did your neighbor say anything about where the soldiers were taking your parents? Did you hear anything at all?" Max shook his head "no."

"It took me two days to get here, because I could only walk at night," Max continued. "In the daytime there were too many soldiers on the road and I was afraid they would see me. I got lost several times." Max sniffled, reaching behind his glasses to rub his eyes. "The Nazis took Mama and Papa and Julia." Over and over again, he repeated this line, as if repeating it would make it real for him.

This was how cousin Max had come to live with Gabi and her mother. And, just as quickly, he had become part of their plan to escape into hiding. Inside the truck, Gabi smiled over at Max. He sat quietly, so unusual for the energetic young boy. But Max had been numb since the day he arrived at Gabi's home. All he could think about were his mother, father, and sister. Where were they? Were they safe? Were they even still alive? He longed to be with them. Gabi and her mother were wonderful and kind, but it was not the same. It could never be the same as living with his own parents. Deep inside, he felt alone and so scared.

Inside the cold truck, Mama took a deep breath and smiled reassuringly at Gabi and Max. "We made it," she said.

Made it where, wondered Gabi. The air was silent and peaceful, interrupted only by a rooster crowing in the distance, the lazy sound of cows mooing from the field in the hills. The sounds of the animals were sharp and crisp in the fresh morning air. Joseph opened the back door of the truck. The sun had just risen and daylight streamed in.

Chapter Two

FATHER LENSKY

"COME OUT, EVERYONE," Joseph whispered, glancing around to make sure no one was nearby. "Leave your bags here. I'll take care of them. Just follow me into the church. Come quickly."

Gabi, Mama, and Max climbed out of the truck, glancing back at their small cases. They had brought one bag each, filled mainly with warm clothes that Mama said they would need. Their sweaters and jackets had taken up most of the space. At the last moment, Max had thrown in several books from Gabi's bookshelf, adventure stories of daring and courage. He kept the one photo of his family close to his chest inside his jacket. It was the only thing he had grabbed when he fled his home. Before leaving her room for the last time, Gabi had agonized over which special keepsake to take with her. She finally settled on the doll that Papa had given her for her tenth birthday. The doll had golden blond hair, the bluest eyes, and real eyelashes. Mama took some family photos that she said would bring her comfort.

Gabi, Mama, and Max barely had a chance to look around as they darted after Joseph down a narrow stone stairway, through a heavy wooden door, and into the back of the town church. Gabi paused as they entered, allowing her eyes to adjust to the sudden darkness. The church was cool, quiet, and serene, reminding her of their synagogue back at home. It had been years since Gabi and the other Jewish families in her town had been allowed to worship in public. Gabi missed the sound of the familiar prayers being chanted.

Gabi had never set foot in a church before and, like a visitor to a new country, she curiously viewed her surroundings. Everywhere around her, from the walls to the pews, deep red wood shone with a luster that came from years of loving care. Two simple stained glass windows allowed in just enough light to create a soft rainbow of colors across the floor, catching particles of dust in its glow. At the front, the altar was adorned with a beautiful red and gold tapestry, spread out over a long table. Gabi sighed. Here in the warmth and simple beauty of this chapel, she felt almost protected.

"Welcome, my visitors. I'm so relieved you're finally here." Gabi and her family turned to face a small, round man walking swiftly toward them. "I'm Father Lensky, the priest here in Olsavica. I thought you would be here much before sunrise. I was so worried."

"Don't worry, Father," said Joseph. "We made it safely and no one followed us."

"Good, good. Mrs. Klein, it is a pleasure to meet you," the priest continued, pumping Mama's hand up and down.

"Father Lensky, we are so grateful to you. You are saving our lives," responded Mama.

The priest shook his head and shrugged. "Nonsense. It's the least that decent people can do when the rest of the world seems to have gone mad. Besides, Joseph is the one you must thank, not me." Gabi looked over at Joseph in gratitude.

Gabi recalled the night Mama and Joseph sat at their kitchen table, putting the final plans for their escape into place. First, Joseph talked about the village where he would take them. Then, he talked about Mr. and Mrs. Kos, the couple with whom they would be hiding. Gabi already knew the Kos family. Mr. Kos had worked for her father for many years, before the law forbidding Christians to work for Jews. Before he left, Mr. Kos had come to Mama and offered to do anything he could to help her in the future. Joseph had contacted Mr. Kos when he was searching for a safe place to take Mama and the family.

Joseph had carefully gone over the details of their escape: when it was safest to leave, how they would travel, and what they could bring. Finally, Mama looked into Joseph's eyes and said, "I am trusting you with my life, Joseph — and with the life of my precious daughter and nephew."

Joseph had looked back at Mama and said, "We are friends. We have lived next to each other for many years. We have worked together. We have shared joyous occasions and sad ones as well. You can trust me. This is what friends do for each other."

Father Lensky moved on to Gabi, reaching up to place his hand on her shoulder. "So, you are young Gabi.

Welcome, my child." When was the last time she had received a greeting as friendly as this, thought Gabi, as she shook the priest's outstretched hand. Finally, Father Lensky turned to Max. "And, you must be Gabi's cousin. It's a pleasure to meet you, Max." Silently and somberly, Max took Father Lensky's hand and shook it.

"In a few minutes, we'll go to the house of Stephan and Maria Kos where you will be staying. I can see that you have removed the stars from your clothing and that's just as well."

The night before, Gabi had sat with her mother, helping to remove the yellow stars of David that all Jews had been forced to sew on every article of clothing they owned. Several years ago, the Nazis had created this law as a way to identify Jews and single them out for mistreatment. Gabi glanced down at her jacket where the outline of a six-pointed star was still faintly visible. Instinctively, she reached up to rub the spot, as if she could wipe out the years of misery she and the other Jewish families had suffered at the hands of the Nazis. It felt good having the star off her jacket. Without it, Gabi felt more free.

"But, I'm afraid you will still have to change out of your clothes," continued Father Lensky. "Dressed as you are, you might easily be spotted as strangers in this village. Strangers are always subject to suspicion. I have some clothing here for you to wear, simple farm clothes that will draw less attention to you." Father Lensky reached down behind one of the pews and pulled out a pile of clothing, handing it to them. For Gabi and her mother, there were long woolen skirts with petticoats to layer underneath. Each of them had a colorful cotton blouse to go with the skirt and a scarf for their heads. Max had a pair of long pants with suspenders, a heavy cotton work shirt, and a peasant's cap for his head.

While they moved to another room to change out of their clothes, Gabi could not help but think about the priest's greeting. He had called them "visitors" rather than fugitives, and said they would be "staying" with the Kos family, not hiding in their home. He made Gabi feel like a guest, not like an escaped refugee. But, Gabi knew that staying in this village was not going to be a holiday. And not everyone here was going to act like a gracious host.

Chapter Three

A SAFE PLACE TO HIDE

Gabi finished tying the scarf around her head and smoothed out her long skirt. When she turned to face her mother, she gasped. She barely recognized the woman in front of her. Mama wore a long, heavy woolen skirt covered with a plain white apron. Her faded cotton blouse was buttoned to her neck and, on her head, she had tied a simple blue handkerchief with frayed edges. The scarf flattened Mama's stylish hair, making her look plain. Mama had always been so fashionable. In her community, she had been known as a refined lady and she always took great pride in her appearance.

Mama smiled in response to Gabi's reaction. She stood up tall and proud in her peasant clothing. "What would our neighbors think of us now, Gabilinka?" Mama asked. "Would they even know who we are?"

Max emerged from the small room behind the altar where he had changed and grinned. "Look Gabi," he said, "I'm a farm boy now." It was the first smile Gabi and her mother had seen from Max in a long time.

"Ah, I see you're ready." Father Lensky reappeared from

another room. "And you look like genuine locals! And now, you must say good-by to Joseph and we'll be on our way to your hiding place."

Joseph approached from the shadows and stood in front of Gabi's family. Mama moved forward, clasping Joseph's hands, embracing him warmly. "Thank you just isn't enough," she whispered. Joseph awkwardly patted Mama's shoulder, looking embarrassed. "There, there, Judith. I'll be back whenever possible with food and other supplies. In the meantime, Father Lensky will take good care of all of you. I'm sure of it."

"I pray this madness will soon be over and we can return to our home," said Mama.

It seemed to Gabi that her mother had been saying the same thing for years. Soon you will be able to return to school. Soon you will be able to play with your old friends. Soon we'll be able to shop in stores and walk on the street. Soon we won't be afraid of being arrested. Soon this and soon that. But so far, nothing had returned to normal. Things had only gotten worse.

Joseph patted Gabi and Max on the head, as he passed them on his way out the door. "Take care of your Mama and of each other." And then he was gone.

Father Lensky wasted no time. "Let me explain how we will do this," he said. "You will not be able to walk to the Kos family home together. Three of you walking together and arriving at once might create too much attention. That's one of the reasons we thought it wiser for Joseph to bring you to the church first. Mrs. Klein, you will go first with me. Then, after a few minutes, Max and Gabi will follow."

"Do you think it is safe for the children to walk alone?" asked Mama.

"Yes," replied Father Lensky. "They are less likely to be bothered on their own. And no one will stop you, Mrs. Klein, if you are with me." He continued with his instructions. "Walk quickly, but don't run. Act naturally. Look straight ahead, as though you know where you are going. Many of the village houses look the same, so pay close attention. It will take you about ten minutes to reach the Kos's farmhouse. They live in the fourth last house from the end of the road, on the left side. It is a small white house with a red fence and gate. Count the houses silently and make sure you have the right one. There will be a red scarf on the gate, just to let you know for sure that you are in the right place. Talk to no one. Try to be invisible. Keep your heads down. We can never be too sure that someone won't be on the lookout to turn a stranger over to the authorities. Is that clear?"

So many instructions, thought Gabi. So many things to remember: a white house, fourth from the end of the road, on the left side, a red gate. What if she miscounted? What if someone stopped them before they reached the right house? How would she make herself invisible? A mass of questions swirled in her head as she nodded silently and moved to the door with Mama and Max. Father Lensky took Mama by the arm and escorted her out first, while Gabi and Max waited nervously inside.

"We'll be okay, Max," said Gabi trying to sound confident in front of Max. "Let's wait five minutes and then we'll go." Silently, Gabi counted the seconds in her head, waiting for five long minutes to pass. Finally, she nodded to Max and pushed open the heavy door of the church. The two of them walked outside into the morning light.

The mountain air was so pure and cold, it almost hurt to breathe it in. But the sun felt good on Gabi's face, warming her shivering body, as she and Max moved onto the road. There was only one road in this tiny village, so that part was easy. Keeping her head down, Gabi moved quickly, holding on to Max's arm and counting the houses silently.

"Don't worry, Max," said Gabi, glancing at the shivering body of her cousin. "We'll be safe."

"Sure we will, Gabi," said Max, taking Gabi's lead.

An old woman passed Gabi and Max on the other side of the road, glanced in the children's direction, but moved on. She looked curious, but friendly enough. Still, Gabi remembered the priest's warning. Talk to no one.

"You know, I remember the time the Nazi soldiers came to our house to search for me," Gabi began, trying to sound reassuring to her young cousin. "My name was on a list with other girls who were being taken away to work in factories. Mama would never allow anyone to take me away from her and she knew that she would have to hide me. So, do you know what I did? I hid in the dining room dresser. We took out all the china and silverware. Then we lowered the shelf to the bottom of the dresser to make a hiding place for me. The soldiers came to the door, demanding to know where I was. They didn't believe Mama when she said I was away visiting relatives. They pushed their way in and almost ripped apart the house, looking for me. They searched every-where in our house, but they never looked inside the dresser. They never found me. I was safe. After the soldiers left and Mama let me out of the dresser, she said to me, 'Someone is watching out for us.' I always remember that. We'll be safe this time too, Max."

Suddenly, Gabi felt Max stiffen next to her. Approaching them on the same side of the road were two uniformed soldiers. The two men were walking easily, with their guns slung casually over their shoulders. They chatted with each other as they walked up the road, glancing at the houses on either side. Their black shiny boots crunched noisily in the snow, as they came closer to Gabi and Max with each step. Gabi stumbled on a rock in the road and began to shake. She pulled Max closer to her as her fear intensified. This was just what Father Lensky said not to do, the voice inside her head screamed. Try to be natural and then they won't notice you. Keep your head down. Look like you belong, not like a stranger. But as much as Gabi ordered her body to remain calm, her panic continued to spread. The soldiers were now directly ahead of Max and Gabi.

"Good morning, children," one of the soldiers said as he stopped in front of the young people and stared down at them. Gabi froze. She couldn't speak.

"Good morning." It was Max who replied.

The soldiers paused, blocking the children's path, and stood staring down at them. "This is early for young children to be out walking. Where have you been?"

Once again, it was Max who spoke. "We've been to the

church, helping the priest." The lie rolled easily out of Max's mouth.

"Well, it's a cold morning to be out," the soldier continued. "You'd be better off inside, where it's warm."

"Thank you, sir. We're on our way home now." With that, Max pulled Gabi by the arm and pushed past the soldiers. Gabi shuddered at the rough touch of the soldier's uniform on her arm when she brushed by him. She felt her head spinning as the soldiers continued up the road and she was grateful to Max for remaining calm.

They continued to walk down the road, but Gabi was still on edge, losing count of the houses. Father Lensky had said it would take ten minutes to reach the Kos farmhouse. It seemed as though hours had passed, since they had left the safety of the church. The houses on both sides of the road looked similar and each had a red fence. They were all small and several of them were white. Which house had they just passed? Was it number seven or number ten? Where was the end of the road? Gabi looked around wildly.

And then, she suddenly caught sight of a red scarf, waving from a red wooden gate ahead like a flag, beckoning them to their destination. They had found the right house. Moving swiftly to open the gate, Gabi and Max walked up to the front door as it opened, inviting them inside.

Chapter Four

THE KOS FARMHOUSE

"COME IN QUICKLY," Father Lensky's voice called urgently from behind the door. The children entered into a small, crowded room and fell into Mama's arms.

"Oh Gabi, Max, I'm so relieved we're all here now," said Mama, squeezing them tightly.

Max looked at Mama. "We saw soldiers, Aunt Judith," he said. "But, it's okay. We got past them." Gabi nodded weakly in agreement.

"Yes," said Father Lensky. "They're known as the Hlinka guard. They are the army here in this part of Czechoslovakia. They are supporters of Adolf Hitler, just as bad as the Nazis and sometimes even worse. Our government acts like a puppet, while Hitler pulls the strings and tells us what to do." Father Lensky spat these words out angrily, then took a deep breath and continued. "The Nazis have been sending soldiers into this area for some time. They say it is for our protection, but we know they are searching for Jews. That's why we must be so cautious."

"Gabi, do you remember Mr. and Mrs. Kos?" Mama interrupted, gesturing toward the elderly couple standing on the other side of the room. "They worked on our farm for so many years, long before any of these troubles began."

"Gabi, my dear, we are so glad to have you in our home," said Stephan Kos, reaching out to shake Gabi's hand and then greeting Max. Mr. Kos's hands were big and rough from years of working on the land. He was a strongly built man, but his manner was gentle and his face was round and soft. And despite his years, Gabi could not help but notice his full head of thick, dark hair. "Your father was a wonderful person," continued Mr. Kos. "Always good to us, generous and kind. It's our pleasure to help you now, just as he helped us so many times."

After greeting Gabi and Max, Mr. Kos turned to introduce his wife. Maria Kos was a small woman with a plain and wrinkled face. Her eyes darted anxiously in all directions, as if she thought someone was watching her. She pulled her wool shawl up over her shoulders and moved closer to Gabi, inspecting her carefully. "You're going to have to be very quiet while you're here. No noise, no sounds. It's dangerous having you here, you know." She didn't seem as welcoming as her husband or Father Lensky, thought Gabi.

"And this is our granddaughter Eva. She lives with us while her mother works in the city," said Mr. Kos. Gabi turned to face the young girl standing in the shadows. Eva was about the same age as Gabi. Her cropped blond hair flew in all directions and her overalls were worn and torn, as if she were accustomed to playing hard. A look of inquisitiveness shone in Eva's sparkling blue eyes. She gazed boldly over at Gabi, inspecting her curiously from head to toe.

"You're Jewish, aren't you?" Eva blurted out, moving her blond hair away from her blue eyes. For a moment Gabi froze. She eyed Eva warily. These days when someone asked your religion so bluntly, it usually meant they were out to harm you.

"Yes," replied Gabi hesitantly. She still felt shaken from her encounter with the Hlinka soldiers.

"Good," said Eva. "My grandfather says that we must help Jewish people. So I guess we will be helping you." Gabi forced a smile and nodded, but still felt uneasy.

"I'm going to have to feed you," continued Mrs. Kos, somewhat reluctantly. "So, you'd better come to the table and eat now. I don't want you starving on me." Gabi suddenly realized how hungry she was. It had been many hours since they had last eaten. She moved to the table with her family and looked around.

The Kos's farmhouse was neat and clean, but tiny. The front room where they had entered served as family room, living room, dining room and kitchen all rolled into one. A comfortable sofa was pushed up against the wall at one end. Small, handmade doilies were scattered across the couch, hiding its worn arms and back. Lace curtains adorned the small window above the sofa. Ornaments, pictures, and other knick-knacks were displayed on rough wooden shelves around the room. A radio held a place of honor on one of those shelves. Radios provided valuable information about the progress of the war. Jews had been forbidden to own them for some time.

They sat down on the wooden benches surrounding the

large wooden dining table in the center of the room. At the other end of the room, a deep basin held dishes next to the pump that Mrs. Kos used to bring in water from the well outside. The tub for bathing and washing clothes was hidden under the basin. Next to it, a giant stove glowed warmly, sputtering and crackling with the sound of wood burning from inside.

Mrs. Kos carried a large blackened soup pot from the stove to the table. With Mama's help, she began to dish out bowls of soup while Mr. Kos sliced thick pieces of black bread. The soup had a heavenly aroma and Gabi hungrily gulped back spoonfuls. There were potatoes, beans, and chunks of onion and carrot, simmered into a thick broth. The bread was still warm from the oven. Gabi was just about to take a second piece when Mrs. Kos interrupted.

"You can see we don't have much," said Mrs. Kos. "It's difficult these days to get food. Whatever we can, we grow and store for winter days like this. But things like sugar, flour, and salt are becoming more and more difficult to find."

Gabi pulled her arm back guiltily, trying to ignore the hunger still rumbling in her stomach. How she longed for the meals her mother used to prepare before the war, on tables groaning from the weight of their feasts. By comparison, the Kos family had so little.

As the others finished eating, Father Lensky began to talk. "So far, the Nazis have not occupied our village. But now this area is becoming more important to them," explained Father Lensky. "They are building a new road outside this village. Men from our village and the surrounding towns are being forced to work on the road. The men labor like animals, day and night. The Nazis plan to use the road to bring in troops and tanks to keep this area under Nazi rule. They are preparing for what we think will be a big battle against the Russians. If the Russians can beat the Nazis in Poland, it will only be a short time before they move into Czechoslovakia and push the Nazis out of here. I pray that we can hold out until the Russians arrive from the east."

Father Lensky continued, "It is very dangerous for Mr. and Mrs. Kos to keep you hidden in their home. If they are discovered hiding a Jewish family, they will be arrested on the spot. And that's if they are lucky. They could be killed for doing this." Gabi's eyes widened. She was beginning to realize just what the Kos family was risking by having them here. They were a poor family, but they had opened up their meager home to Gabi and her family at a time when so many others were not even willing to acknowledge Jews on the street. Maybe that's why Mrs. Kos seemed so nervous.

"Father, please stop. You're scaring the children," interrupted Mr. Kos.

"I know the things that can happen and I'll try not to be scared," said Max, as Gabi reached over protectively to put her arm around his shoulder.

"Good," responded Father Lensky. "You will need to be brave, but also very wise. I must speak frankly because you need to be aware of all the dangers. We are glad to have you here in our village. We are doing what decent people everywhere should do. But we also know the risks involved. And you must know them as well. For the most part, you will not be allowed to go outside, unless you are given permission. Is that understood?" Gabi, Mama, and Max all nodded solemnly. "In the daytime, you must be quiet and remain in hiding. These walls are thin and the road runs only a few feet away. Soldiers often pass by and could hear you. Even the neighbors must not know you are here. I would like to believe that the people of this town are all kindhearted. But these days it is hard to know what people might do out of fear. Anyone could report you to the authorities, and report Mr. and Mrs. Kos as well. So, that's why we must be so careful. Perhaps we are being too cautious," he said, noting the strained expression on Gabi's face. "But we want to protect your lives and ours."

"Tell them they must stay in the barn all the time, Stephan," said Mrs. Kos. "Tell them they can't come out during the day, not at all."

Mr. Kos patted his wife's arm. "During the day, neighbors drop by unexpectedly," he said. "Not everyone would be happy to see a Jewish family in our midst. But at night, you can come out of hiding and join us here in the house."

"We'll have to make sure the curtains are drawn at night and we'll keep the lights low, so no one can see you," added Mrs. Kos.

"Now that you have finished eating, I must show you where you will be sleeping and spending most of your time," said Mr. Kos. "Come. I'll take you into the barn."

Leading the way, Mr. Kos moved down a narrow hallway past one side of the room. He motioned the family to follow. Single file, they proceeded down the hall toward the back of the house.

Gabi walked by the Kos's bedroom with its feather comforter and down-filled pillows piled on the big canopy bed. Past the bedroom at the end of the hallway hung a plain canvas curtain. As Mr. Kos pulled the curtain aside, Gabi and Max gasped as they realized the most amazing thing about this house. Beyond the curtain, the house turned into a barn. Suddenly, the wooden floors were covered with hay. The house and the barn were in fact one continuous space, broken up only by a simple drape hanging from the ceiling.

Gabi stepped into the barn and inhaled its familiar odor. It smelled sweet and damp at the same time, just like the barn at home. In fact, all the smells and sounds of the barn were familiar — chickens scratching in the hay for seeds, ducks cackling in a low harmony. Here and there, barn cats stretched lazily, purring with contentment as rays of sunlight streamed in through the holes in the ceiling and caught them in their beams. The cows were out grazing on the hillside and would return in the evening.

Gabi bent to scratch the head of a fat yellow cat as it pushed its big head up against her leg. How well fed you look, she thought enviously. There must be plenty of mice and bugs around to keep this cat looking so healthy. Max coughed as dust and bits of dirt floated down from the ceiling and covered them all like fine snowflakes. He pulled his jacket tightly around his neck to protect himself from the wind that whistled in through the open slits and cracks in the wall. It was a small barn, just big enough to house Mr. Kos's twenty cows. And now it would have to accommodate three new "guests" as well.

Mr. Kos pointed to a small ladder at the far end of the barn leading to a hayloft. "You'll be staying up there," he said and moved forward to climb the narrow steps. Gabi, Mama, and Max followed. At the top of the ladder were bales of hay, tightly wrapped, and piled in neat mounds. With little effort, Mr. Kos pushed one of the bales aside, revealing what looked like a narrow tunnel to the back of the hayloft.

Mr. Kos sounded apologetic and lowered his eyes as he spoke. "It's terrible that you must hide in a barn with the animals, but we think it will be safe," he said, motioning inside the tunnel. "We've packed together these bundles of hay to build your hiding place. You won't be able to stand up in there, but there is space to stretch out and sleep. My wife has put blankets inside for you."

"As long as we're safe," said Mama, simply. "That is what's most important."

"During the day, you should have enough light coming in from the holes in the walls of the barn," continued Mr. Kos. "We can't risk having a lantern in there. Neighbors might see the glow."

So much thought had gone into preparing this place for them, thought Gabi. She was grateful and hoped they had thought of everything.

"I have one more thing to say, Mrs. Klein," said Mr. Kos, turning to face Mama. "My wife is a good woman and in her heart she knows we are doing the right thing to have you here. But she has bad nerves. Don't mistake her behavior for lack of caring."

"You mustn't apologize for your wife," said Mama, simply. "We are all scared." Mama stood up tall. "And please call me Judith. No more formalities, Stephan. We're in this together."

With that, Mama bent over to crawl into the hiding space, followed by Max and Gabi. Gabi grimaced as she bent to follow Max. She held her breath and squeezed her eyes shut, as she flung herself through the tunnel. She prayed that no barn rat or creeping bug would bite her as she crawled through. The prickly hay pressed through the fabric of her skirt and into her knees.

When she emerged on the other side, Gabi took a deep breath and looked around. Bales of hay were stacked neatly, one on top of another, above her head and surrounding her on three sides of the hiding space. The fourth side was the outer wall of the barn. Light filtered in from slits in the barn wall. Gabi knew the light wouldn't last long. Once night fell, they would not only be sealed up inside the barn, but they would be encased in darkness. How were the three of them ever going to be able to stay in this tiny space, without suffocating or going crazy? It was six feet wide, six feet long, and about four feet high. That was the total amount of space allotted to her family — enough to sit or lie down, but no room to stand. It was a straw cave, a fort made of hay, no bigger than one of her closets back at home.

"We'll come to get you when it's safe to come out for the evening," called Mr. Kos from the other side of the tunnel. "I'll try to check on you from time to time, if I can."

With that, Gabi heard the loose bale of hay being replaced and Mr. Kos descending the ladder on the other side.

Gabi, Mama, and Max stared silently at their new "home."

Chapter Five

THE HAYLOFT

MAMA SPOKE FIRST. "Come, children. Let's arrange our space." Blankets were piled neatly in one corner of the hiding place. Mr. Kos, or perhaps Joseph, had already placed their cases with their few belongings in another corner. Mama quickly took charge, distributing the blankets and handing out their extra clothing from the suitcases. It was difficult to get organized in the tight space.

"Ouch!" yelled Max. Gabi had accidentally swatted him while pulling a sweater over her head. Max rubbed his arm. "Watch what you're doing."

"I'm sorry, Max," said Gabi. "I didn't mean to punch you. Just move your leg over so I can stretch out."

"I can't move any further," complained Max as he squirmed and shoved Gabi's arm aside. "Look, I'm already pushed up against this pile of hay."

Already Gabi felt the straw closing in on her, as she crouched over to avoid banging her head.

"Children, stop it," interrupted Mama. "Max, move your leg to this side and that way Gabi can stretch out next to you. I know it's snug, but we have to work together and help each other."

Gabi shook her head and sighed. There was nothing snug about this place. Snug was her bed at home when she buried herself under her thick feather comforter. Snug was how she felt when Mama used to build a fire in the wood stove of their kitchen and her cheeks burned in its blaze. This hiding place was not snug. It was bleak and unwelcoming.

"Fine," said Max, shifting his body. He drew an imaginary line in the hay around his legs and shoulders, claiming one corner of the hiding place. "This is my space and that's yours. Don't put your legs in my space, Gabi."

Gabi shifted over, as well, and shivered. The bales of hay surrounding them on three sides provided some warmth. But the temperature outside had dropped to below zero and cold air whistled in through the slits of the fourth barn wall. Mama shoved their empty cases up against the wooden wall, and pushed some hay into the larger cracks, to block the wind from gusting through. But it didn't help. Max's teeth chattered loudly as he draped a pair of trousers around his neck and wound a scarf over his head. He looked almost comical. So did Gabi, as she wrapped a sweater around each of her feet and her shoulders.

Gabi, Max, and Mama stared at each other again. Now what do we do, thought Gabi. It was only mid-day. It would be hours before they could leave the barn.

"I think we should try to get some sleep," said Mama. "We were up so early this morning and I, for one, am exhausted. Besides," she continued as if reading Gabi's mind, "sleeping will help pass the time. Before we know it, Mr. Kos will return to bring us into the house for the evening."

Gabi burrowed deep into the soft hay floor, careful to avoid Max's space. She could already see how hard it was going to be not to get on each other's nerves. Max and Mama stretched out beside her, each one piling mounds of hay over their legs and arms. Their breaths mingled together in the small space above their heads. The sound of their inhaling and exhaling seemed suddenly so loud in the stillness of the hiding place. Gabi could hear shouts from outside — farmers on the hill or children going about their day. She startled as squeaky sounds came from inside the barn. Was that the barn door or a barn mouse? Was that Mrs. Kos sweeping or Mr. Kos working in the yard?

Max moved restlessly beside her and then jumped as a spider crawled up his arm and disappeared somewhere into his jacket. He punched and pounded his shoulder hoping he'd killed it or that it had gotten lost somewhere in the stacks of hay.

Gabi closed her eyes to sleep, but her mind was still racing. How was this rickety old barn ever going to keep them safe, she wondered, pulling her sweater tighter around her neck. And how long were they going to have to stay here? A month? A year? This war had already lasted so much longer than anyone had predicted.

Gabi pulled her doll close to her. Its porcelain face was ice cold, but that didn't matter. It was good just to hold the doll, to cradle it in her arms, and to think about home. Gabi longed for the home that she had left behind. She worried about her friends and wondered where they were and if they were in danger. She thought about Mama and how desperate she was to keep her family safe. And finally, she imagined her father. I wish so much that he were here with us, prayed Gabi. And with that thought, Gabi finally surrendered to sleep.

Chapter Six

MAX

MAX AWOKE BEFORE Gabi and Mama. For a moment, he lay quietly in the cold stillness of the barn, watching his frozen breath curl up and dissolve into the uneven bales of hay above him. He put on his glasses to look around. From the color of the light, filtering through the barn wall, Max guessed that it was nearing the end of the day. There was some sunlight left, but it was quickly fading.

Max took out the photograph of his family from deep inside his jacket, smoothing out its crinkled edges and staring at the smiling faces of his parents and sister. If he had been home right now, his father would be returning from work in his bookstore and his mother would be making supper. He and his sister would start their homework and probably begin their squabbling, as brother and sister often did. Max slid the picture back inside his jacket and shut his eyes tight, trying to block the memories of his family. It hurt too much to think of them. The pain felt like it was making a hole in his heart. He thought about the soldiers that he and Gabi had met on the short walk to the Kos's house. Soldiers like that had arrested his parents. Gabi thought he had been so bold by speaking up to the soldiers. But really, he was more angry than brave.

Mama began to stir next to Max and opened her eyes, looking around uncertainly before remembering where she was. She smiled at Max and then looked over at Gabi, still asleep and buried in the hay.

"Shhh," she whispered. "We'll let her sleep. Come, Max. I think it's dark enough now for us to go inside the house."

Max moved the bale of hay aside to expose the tunnel, letting his aunt go first before he moved outside the hiding place and into the barn. The two of them descended the ladder from the hayloft to the barn, walked past the animals, and cautiously pushed the curtain aside, as they walked into the house. Max welcomed the sudden blast of warm air that wafted down the hallway. It became much warmer as Mama and Max made their way into the kitchen.

Mr. Kos was the first to greet them. "I was just coming to get you," he said, cordially.

"Next time, you must wait for my husband," said Mrs. Kos, fidgeting with her apron and rushing to draw the curtains across the kitchen windows. "You can't leave the barn on your own, you know."

"I'm sorry, Maria," said Mama. "You're right. Next time we will wait."

Mrs. Kos is mean, thought Max. She reminded him of some of their neighbors at home, the ones who didn't like the Jews. Mrs. Kos did not seem to like them being here, regardless of her husband's excuses for her.

"Where's Gabi?" asked Eva.

"She's still sleeping," answered Max. He was curious about Eva. She looked like a tomboy and he liked that about her. He saw a ball in the corner and realized she played soccer, his favorite sport. She could probably show him things on the farm that would be fun — that is, if he were ever allowed to do fun things again.

"I'm going to get Gabi," said Eva, moving toward the hallway.

"If she's still sleeping, don't wake her, Evichka," said Mr. Kos. Mama nodded in agreement as Eva left the room. "And you, Max," continued Mr. Kos, "would you like to come outside and gather some wood with me? We need more wood to keep the stove going."

"No, Stephan," said Mrs. Kos, anxiously, as her eyes darted around the room. "I don't think the boy should leave the house."

"Are you sure it's safe, Stephan?" asked Mama.

Mr. Kos glanced through the curtain of the kitchen window. "It's quite dark now. That's the only safe time to be outside. The men are back home from the fields and the women are all indoors, cooking. We'll stay in the yard close to the house and we won't be too long. It will be fine, Maria. Stop worrying."

Reluctantly, Mrs. Kos wrapped a knit scarf around Max's head and handed him a pair of mittens. Then, with a wave of her hand, she pushed him out the door with her husband.

Outside, the cold air caught Max's breath. He paused

for one moment, and then, without a second thought, he bounded into the air, feeling the snowflakes melt across his nose and cheeks. Max darted across the farmyard and kicked the snow up over his head, delighted as it cascaded down over him. The winter air was fresh and crisp. Max closed his eyes and breathed in deeply. It felt so good to be outdoors.

Mr. Kos waited a minute, watching as the young boy frolicked in the fresh air, enjoying Max's newfound energy. Then he called out to Max and together they crossed the yard toward the back of the farmhouse. Piles of split wood were neatly stacked against the back wall — a mountain of wood, enough to last until the end of the winter. Mr. Kos walked over to the woodpile and began handing logs to Max.

"We'll have that fire in the stove blazing in no time," said Mr. Kos.

Max nodded, struggling under the weight of the wood. Max liked Mr. Kos. He was kind and friendly. "I can help with chores around the farm," said Max. "I can take the cows out, chop wood, or even plow the field. I'm pretty strong, you know."

Mr. Kos nodded. "I can see that you are. There's nothing I'd like more than to have you help me, but I'm afraid that won't be possible." Seeing the dejection in Max's eyes, Mr. Kos added quickly, "You have an important job here, Max. You must stay with your aunt and with Gabi. You have to help them."

Max lowered his head. Maybe if he had stayed with his parents and sister, he might have protected them. But he knew this was unlikely.

"We'll do everything we can to keep you safe, Max," said Mr. Kos as if reading Max's mind.

Max blinked and looked up at Mr. Kos. In the last few days, Max had met people who wanted to help him: Joseph who brought them up to the village, Father Lensky who brought them to this farmhouse, and now Mr. Kos who was willing to hide them. This kind of generosity was so rare. Max looked up at Mr. Kos. "Most of the people back in my town hated Jews. And even if they didn't hate us, they wouldn't want to help us. It's too dangerous."

Mr. Kos looked at Max a long time before replying. "I remember a time when my family was in trouble," he said. "Our harvest had been so poor that season and I didn't think I would have enough money to feed my wife and Evichka. I was working for Mr. Klein, Gabi's father, living on his farm during the week and then returning here to my family on weekends. I went to him and told him my situation. He said to me, 'Stephan, I will give you the money you need.' He was willing to help me. I'll never forget that. We had to stop working for Mr. Klein's farm when Christians were no longer allowed to work for Jews. But I never forgot that man's generosity. Yes, it is dangerous for us to hide you here. But we'll take the risk."

It sounded so simple when Mr. Kos spoke, thought Max. If someone like Mr. Kos had been there to help his parents, maybe he would still be with them.

"Come, Max. Your aunt will start to worry about us if we stay out here any longer. Not to mention what my wife will think."

Chapter Seven

EVA

GABI HAD NO IDEA how long she had slept. At one point, she was vaguely aware of Mr. Kos coming into their hiding place, bringing food with him. He carried bread and some tea. Mama roused her from her sleep, urging her to eat something. Gabi swallowed a few bites and then collapsed again into the soft and prickly hay. She was exhausted, worn out from running and hiding, but even more weary from the never-ending fear.

It was somewhere in that sleepy place just before awakening, that Gabi's mind drifted to another time and place. She was running through the fields behind her house, playing a game with her friends. Her friend Marishka was there, along with her friends Nettie and Jeremy. They were chasing each other, seeing who could run the fastest. Jeremy was in the lead, but he stopped to wait up for Gabi. Gabi liked that and she liked Jeremy. Everyone in the field was laughing and shouting. The sun was shining and its heat moved through Gabi's body like a fire on a cool evening, blanketing her in warmth. She pressed her face up to the sun, allowing its dazzling rays to bathe her cheeks, forehead, eyes, and nose as she sank down into the fields of hay, stretched and rolled over. At the same time, Gabi stretched and opened her eyes to her real world.

A last ray of light sifted through the bales of hay above her and then disappeared. Prickly hay scratched Gabi's cheeks and neck, as she finally turned her head.

"I thought you'd never wake up." Startled, Gabi rolled over to sit up and face Eva who had been sitting cross-legged on the opposite side of the hiding space, curiously staring at Gabi for some time. "Do you have any idea how long you've been sleeping?"

Gabi shook her head. "Where's Mama and Max?" She was still a bit dazed. The light in the barn was fading quickly. Soon it would be pitch black.

"You've slept for hours," continued Eva. "I've been waiting forever. My grandfather said I couldn't wake you. He said you needed the sleep. But I didn't want to wait any longer. So I came to the hayloft. I like your doll," she added. "I have a couple of dolls with cloth faces, not china like yours."

Gabi pulled the doll closer to her chest and stared back at Eva. "Where's ..."

"They're in the house with my grandmother. She's probably feeding them again. There's not much food, but still she feeds everybody with whatever we've got."

Gabi smiled briefly. "That's just like my Mama. Before my father died, our house was always filled with people and my mother would always feed everyone, too." Gabi remembered all the times their house had been full of family and guests, all enjoying Mama's hospitality. Those days seemed very far away.

"My father also died," said Eva. "But, that was when I was a baby, so I don't remember him. How did your father die?"

Still half asleep, Gabi struggled with Eva's bold questions. She swallowed painfully at the mention of her father. "So, where's your mother?" Gabi asked, bringing the attention back to Eva.

"She works in the city, taking care of a rich family. You were rich too, weren't you? I mean, that's what my grandfather said when he used to work on your farm."

Gabi squirmed at this next question and pulled her feet up under her heavy wool skirt. She and Eva were different in so many ways — their personalities, their backgrounds, their religions. But none of that mattered right now. Right now, she was hiding in Eva's family's barn, eating the food at her grandparents' table, and probably wearing some of Eva's clothes.

"Anyway," continued Eva. "I can't stay with my mother, so that's why I stay here with my grandparents. It's okay though. I can visit my mother on holidays."

Gabi fell silent, eyeing Eva cautiously.

"There were a few Jewish girls in my class, but they're gone now," Eva continued. "They were arrested by the Hlinka soldiers. All the Jewish families were. Now the Nazis are building a road nearby so more of their soldiers can get here." Gabi nodded as Eva repeated what Father Lensky had told them. "My grandmother says that more Nazi soldiers will come to our village soon. But I don't think they will. The Jews have all been taken away already — well, at least the ones they knew about. So why would the soldiers want to come back?"

Gabi shifted nervously as Eva continued talking. "My friend said that once they arrest the Jews, it probably means they'll be killed. Do you know anyone who's been arrested?"

Gabi nodded, reluctantly.

"I have this one Jewish friend," said Eva. "Her name is Julia. I used to play at her house, until I wasn't allowed anymore. I saw her being arrested. The soldiers had rifles and went from house to house, checking their lists, picking up Jewish families, and taking them to this big truck parked in front of the church. Most of the village came out to watch. I don't remember seeing Julia cry, but it was all very sad. I wanted to wave to her, but my grandmother said no. She thought I'd get into trouble if I did. So, I just watched Julia leave. Did you ever watch any of your friends being arrested?"

Gabi almost screamed out loud. Of course she had seen friends arrested — and knew that most of them were gone even if she hadn't witnessed their arrest. Marishka, Nettie, and Jeremy — all the friends in her dream — were gone, fleeing for their lives or taken away by force. Either way, Gabi knew nothing of their whereabouts. One time, she sneaked out of the house and watched a truck arrive in the center of her own village. Jewish families were being rounded up and loaded onto the truck. Gabi recognized her friend Sandor and his parents among those arrested. Sandor's mother was wailing to the crowd, begging someone to save her son. But, of course, no one moved, not even Gabi who watched helplessly as the truck pulled away. Mama had been furious with Gabi for leaving the house.

"Hey," continued Eva. "I asked you a question."

"You seem to ask a lot of questions about Jewish people," said Gabi, clearing the lump from her throat. There was something about Eva that disturbed her. Maybe it was the blunt way she spoke or her curiosity about Jews. Whatever it was, Gabi wasn't sure she fully trusted Eva. And she certainly didn't like her questions.

"Come on," said Eva, moving toward the opening in the hay. "I'm supposed to bring you inside when you're up."

Gabi held her breath again and crawled after Eva through the hay tunnel and down the wooden ladder. The cows were in the back of the barn and mooed softly as Eva paused to stroke several of them, before pushing the curtain aside and walking into the house.

"Ah, Gabi, you're finally awake." Mama greeted Gabi as she and Eva entered the warm kitchen. Mama was peeling potatoes at the sink, next to Mrs. Kos. A moment later, the door opened and in walked Max and Mr. Kos, each carrying armfuls of firewood. Max clapped his hands together and rubbed his arms to warm up from the cold.

"It's freezing out there," Mr. Kos said, smiling at Gabi as he stamped his feet. He took off his woolen hat, exposing his full head of hair.

The family sat down to another meal of soup with potatoes and leftover bread. This time there was less than there had been earlier. Gabi ate ravenously, barely looking up, as she tried to fill her empty stomach. But at the end of the meal, she was still hungry.

"Evichka, take Gabi with you and go outside to get some fresh air," said Mr. Kos. "You can spend some time together, before Gabi and Max go back to the hayloft."

"They need to go back now, Stephan," said Mrs. Kos, agitated. "They've been out long enough."

"Perhaps we should go back to the barn now, Stephan," said Mama. "Maria is right. We don't want to take unnecessary chances."

"You see," nodded Mrs. Kos, pacing anxiously in the kitchen. "They need to go back to the barn. Tell them to go back now."

She can't even look at us, thought Gabi.

Once again, it was left to Mr. Kos to calm his wife. "Maria, please," he said, evenly. "The girls need this time to get some exercise. Max and I were outside and no one saw us. No one will see the girls either. I'll watch them through the kitchen window. If I think there's any danger, I'll bring them in immediately."

Mrs. Kos started to speak again and then stopped. Instead, she just stood in the middle of the kitchen, rubbing her hands and fidgeting with her apron. Mama finally broke the awkward silence. "Come, Maria. Let me help you with the dishes." Mama walked toward the basin, as Gabi and Eva put on their coats, scarves, and gloves and headed outside.

The cold air took Gabi's breath away. Max was right. It was freezing, but not the same kind of painful chill that they had felt in the barn. Here outside, in the open air, the cold was fresh and welcome. Gabi dropped her head back and looked up at the sky. The first stars were appearing, bright dots of crystal light that matched the flickering glow of lights coming from the houses in the distance. The smell of burning wood reached Gabi's nostrils. She imagined the families of the village sitting down to their dinners at the end of a long day.

"Hey, watch out!" Eva shouted. Gabi turned, as an armful of snow cascaded over her head like a waterfall. Eva laughed and stooped to scoop up another armful of snow. Gabi sputtered and then bent to gather up some snow herself. The two girls squealed as they thrashed snow at one another. Snowball after snowball came flying, fast and furious. Gabi ducked and crouched, dodging to avoid being hit. Finally, the two girls collapsed in the snow, side by side, breathing heavily in the cold air.

"I can't remember when I had a snowball fight like that," laughed Gabi. "That was so much fun."

Eva propped herself up on one elbow and turned to look at Gabi. "I'm glad you're here," she said. "It's nice to have a friend."

Gabi swallowed hard. She missed her friends from home. She stared back at Eva, but didn't respond. Eva confused her. One minute she seemed suspicious and then the next minute she was friendly and open. Who was the real Eva?

"Wait here," said Eva suddenly, as she stood and bolted for the house. A moment later, she emerged carrying a camera. "It's my grandfather's," she said. "He got it from a Jewish family when the law came out saying they weren't allowed to keep luxuries like this anymore. Instead of giving it to the Nazis, the family gave it to my grandfather. Stand in front of the barn. I want to take a picture of you," she said.

Gabi hesitated a moment. She wasn't sure if having her picture taken was a good thing to do. What if someone else saw it and recognized her?

"Go on," said Eva. "You must see yourself in those clothes. The picture will be a souvenir for you to remember the time you stayed here." Eva spoke as though this were some kind of holiday, as if their stay would soon be over. Yet, this was only her first day in hiding. Gabi moved toward the outer wall of the barn, their refuge.

The only comforting aspect was that Mr. Kos owned the camera. He was the one person, aside from Joseph and Father Lensky, whom Gabi trusted. He wouldn't let a photograph fall into the wrong hands. She'd have to wait and see about trusting Eva.

"Come on," said Eva. "Smile."

Gabi slowly turned to face the camera. This wasn't a vacation and she wasn't a trophy for Eva. Still, she seemed to have no choice. There, in front of the barn, she stared into the camera absently, as Eva clicked the shot.

Chapter Eight

February 1944

THE LETTER

IT SNOWED FOR THE next three weeks. Gabi watched through a thin hole in the barn wall as fat snowflakes tumbled down in endless succession. At times, when the wind shifted, a cloud of flakes would drift in through the cracks in the wood. Gabi caught them on the tip of her finger, watching as their beautiful shapes melted into tiny watery puddles. Days passed. Endless, monotonous days with nothing to do except catch snowflakes and sleep.

"I'm going crazy in here," said Max, one afternoon.

"Hush, Max," replied Mama. "Read a book or play a game."

"But I've read my books three times already. I know them by heart." Max kicked his feet in frustration, sending a spray of hay over Gabi's head.

"Hey, stop it," she snapped. "Stay on your own side." Gabi's nerves were on edge, ready to break at the slightest provocation.

"I don't want to stay anywhere. Stop telling me what to do!"

"Well, stop yelling at me. I didn't do anything to you!"

"Children, quiet, both of you!" Mama whispered, tensely. "You can't shout in here. Someone might hear us. The barn is right beside the road. You must stop fighting!"

But Gabi wanted to shout. She wanted to scream, to howl, to sing, to do anything to break the tension and the monotony. How much longer would they have to stay here? How many more days and weeks of silence could she bear? How could doing nothing all day make her so tired? But she knew the answer to that. Boredom drove you crazy, boredom mixed with hunger and a healthy dose of fear. Still, she reminded herself, what was the alternative? To surrender to the Nazis, to go to a prison, to be killed?

"If my parents were here everything would be different," said Max, furiously. "Everyone keeps telling me what to do. Nobody cares about me." Max wiped away angry tears as Gabi looked on. How could she be so selfish, she thought. At least, Gabi had her mother with her in this hiding place. Max had no idea where his parents were.

Gabi sighed. "Read to me, Max," she said, moving over next to her cousin. Anything to pass the time would help.

Max took a deep breath and began to read from his book *Moby Dick*. Gabi closed her eyes and settled once more into the deep hay as Max read the story of the one-legged ship's captain who seeks vengeance on the huge white whale that has crippled him. They were just getting to the part in the story when Captain Ahab sails away to hunt for the great white whale, when Gabi heard sounds from the other end of the tunnel.

"That must be Mr. Kos," said Max, throwing the bale of hay aside and practically shouting into the tunnel. "Is it time to come out now, Mr. Kos?"

Mama scowled and tugged at Max's sleeve. "Max, I've told you before," she whispered urgently, "you mustn't shout. You've got to wait to see who's there before opening the passageway." It was no use, thought Gabi. Max might as well invite every stranger from the village into their hiding place.

But it wasn't a stranger. It was Mr. Kos telling them to come into the house. "Joseph is here with some supplies," he whispered, as Gabi, Max, and Mama crawled out of their hiding place. "And he's brought a letter for you, Judith."

"I wonder who it's from. How long have we been here now? A month? I haven't received a letter in so long." Mama quickly descended the ladder and moved into the house. Warm air blasted from the wood stove in the kitchen. Mrs. Kos shuffled around the room, staring at Max and Gabi nervously. Joseph greeted all of them warmly.

"I've brought something special," Joseph said to Gabi and Max. "Eva will show you. And for you, Judith, come sit at the table and read your letter. We have much to talk about."

Gabi and Max turned to Eva, who sat on the sofa in the darkened corner of the main room and smiled mysteriously. She beckoned to Gabi and Max who moved over to where they could have a more private conversation.

"Look what I have," said Eva. She reached into her pocket and withdrew a small paper packet and began to unwrap it. Gabi and Max didn't have to wait long to discover what was inside.

"It's chocolate," cried Max. "I know what it is. I can smell it."

He was right. Eva uncovered a small bar of dark chocolate and held it up, like a fragile piece of glass, for the other two to see. "Joseph actually brought it just for me. He said so."

Gabi and Max waited expectantly. What was Eva going to do with this prize?

"But I have decided to share it with the two of you." Gabi and Max let their breaths out slowly.

"Oh, thank you, Eva," said Max. "Will you divide it up?"

Eva nodded and began to break the chocolate bar into three pieces. She carefully measured each piece against the others, making sure they were exactly the same size. Then she passed one to Gabi and one to Max, keeping the last piece for herself.

Gabi took the portion of chocolate and held it up to her nose, inhaling deeply as memories from home flooded through her mind. "The last time I had chocolate was more than two years ago," she whispered. "It was Friday night and we were having Sabbath dinner at our home. Max, you were there with your family and you brought us a box of the best chocolates. Do you remember that?" She turned to look at Max, who had already devoured his segment. Max nodded absently, licking the last flakes of chocolate from his fingers. Gabi turned back to her own portion. Delighting in the moment, she broke off a tiny piece and put it in her mouth, letting it melt slowly across her tongue. Then she turned gratefully to Eva.

Eva always did this to her, Gabi thought. One minute, Gabi was suspicious of Eva's intentions. And the next minute, Gabi liked Eva and was even grateful to her.

"So, what's it like being in the barn all the time?" asked Eva. "I think I'd go crazy, if I had to stay inside all the time."

Max and Gabi nodded. It was impossible to explain what it felt like to do nothing and be confined to a small space where one could not even stand up. "I saw you playing soccer in the field on the hill," said Max. "I watched through a slit in the wall. If I squint hard, I can see the meadow on the hill, right in front of the woods, and I can watch the game. I would give anything to be outside, running on that hill — just for few minutes. That's all I want. That and some more chocolate." Gabi smiled at Max. He certainly was annoying at times. But she couldn't imagine being here without him.

"Next time I'm playing soccer, I'll signal to you, Max, like this." Eva began to scratch the top of her head with her fingertips. "It will be my secret signal. I'll try to score a goal for you."

Max grinned. "And I'll pretend I'm on the field with you, Eva. I'll run ahead of you, and trip all the other players so you can score."

Eva turned to look at Gabi. "What would you do right now, if you could get out of this place?" she asked.

Gabi thought hard. "If I could do anything, I'd love to be skating again. No, wait. I'd be skiing or maybe I'd just be in school. Oh, I don't know. There are too many things to pick just one."

Behind the children, at the table, Mama was having an animated conversation with Joseph and Mr. Kos. Gabi whirled around when her mother suddenly let out a low cry.

"Mama, what's wrong?" asked Gabi. Her mother had suddenly gone pale. In her hands, she clutched the letter Joseph had brought.

"I can't stand what is happening," she cried to Joseph. "It's too much to think about." Mama pounded her fist angrily on the table. And then she was overcome with grief. The tears, long bottled up and hidden from anyone, flowed down her cheeks like rainwater pouring down an eaves trough. Mama covered her face with her trembling hands.

"Mama, tell me what's wrong." Gabi rushed toward the table, alarmed at her mother's anguish. Gabi had never seen her mother like this before. Mama was always so strong and in control. Mama was the one who had hidden her in the dresser and carefully planned their flight into this village. Mama always took charge. Suddenly, she seemed fragile and it startled Gabi to see her mother's fear.

Mama sat up, trying hard to compose herself. She wiped the tears from her cheeks and hesitated. "The letter is from Germany — from my cousin Magda. I had heard that Magda had been arrested by the Nazis in her town of Frankfurt," said Mama. "All the Jews of Frankfurt were told they had a day to pack a few belongings and report to their train station for 'relocation.' They were being sent to a concentration camp where they would work. Before Magda left her apartment, she gave this letter to a neighbor, a woman who had been kind to her and to other Jews. This woman contacted a friend of Joseph, who passed the letter on to him. The letter was written more than a month ago. It has traveled so long and so far, bringing this terrible news." Mama handed the crumpled letter to her daughter.

"Read it out loud," Mama said. "There's no use hiding this from either of you." She nodded to Gabi and pointed to a place in the letter. "Read from here." Gabi looked down at the letter, took a deep breath, and began to read:

"... my dear Judith, I won't be able to write to you again. This will probably be the last time. So many others have been sent on vacation, my mother, father, and brother, along with the others. We'll probably be joining them ..."

Gabi looked up, puzzled. "I don't understand, Mama."

"Don't you see, Gabi? Magda's mother, father, and brother are all dead! They died several years ago. Magda is telling me she is being sent away to die as well! That's what this letter is about. It is a warning that she and all the other Jews that were arrested and sent away by train will probably be killed." Mama's voice broke again and she fell silent.

"We should all have left sooner," Mama said, weeping quietly. "We should have gotten out of this country when we could. I've tried to make the best decisions for us, but I'm afraid I've failed. Now, it's too late and I just don't know anymore what will happen to us in the end."

"But we're safe here, Mama," said Gabi. "We're still

healthy and strong and I can help do anything we need." Gabi encircled her mother's shoulders and hugged her tightly.

"Besides," continued Max. "If it weren't for you, Aunt Judith, where would I be right now? You're the only family I have." The letter from Magda terrified Max, even though he was trying hard not to show it. Perhaps his family was among those being sent to their death.

"Gabi is right, Judith," continued Joseph. "You are safest here with Mr. and Mrs. Kos. And you must believe that the war will end soon and Hitler will be defeated. Just last month, we heard on the radio that the Russian troops had reached the Polish border. Soon they will reclaim land that was captured by the Nazis. These are good signs."

Gabi struggled with what she was hearing. From listening to his small radio, Mr. Kos provided daily radio reports to Gabi and her family. Some reports came from Germany and boasted about Hitler's victories. On very clear nights, however, radio reports could be heard from as far away as England and those told of Nazi defeats. Mr. Kos said those were the ones to believe and he always spoke hopefully about the progress of the war. On the other hand, his reports included information about prisons and concentration camps where Jews were being deported by the thousands, day after day. These reports were confusing. Some claimed that Jews were being sent to work in other parts of the country. Other reports told about Jews being put to death in the camps. This letter from Magda stated all too clearly what everyone was most afraid to believe.

Mama reached out for Max's hand. "I'm sorry, children. I don't mean to complain." Frantically, she dried her eyes and wiped her nose. "I think I'm just tired of the fear." I am too, thought Gabi as Max nodded silently.

Mama pressed Gabi to her and kissed her silently on the forehead. "But I am so glad we have each other." She reached out to hold Max's hand.

Gabi sighed and closed her eyes. A moment ago, they had been savoring the taste of fine chocolate. They had been talking about soccer and skating. Then, once again, the realities of war had set in. How had the world become so crazy, she wondered. Why were Jewish people so hated? They used to be children and mothers and teachers and doctors. Now, they were just Jews — and Jews were considered "problems" to be gotten rid of.

"Let's sit down to eat," said Mr. Kos, breaking the silence in the room. "Let's be grateful we are all safe, so far."

Chapter Nine

THE NIGHT WALK

"GABI, WAKE UP," Max whispered in her ear. It was very late at night and Gabi struggled to open her eyes. The endless days had pushed her into a tedious routine. She often slept in the daylight hours to pass the time, waking only to take a bite of a cracker or some bread before trying to sleep some more. Evenings in the house provided the only relief and entertainment. Then, she and Max would talk with Eva or play a quiet game.

"What do you want, Max? Go back to sleep." Gabi rolled over and pulled the blankets higher over her shoulders.

Max shook her once more. "I can't sleep and I don't want to be in here anymore. I'm going outside. Come with me."

Gabi's eyes jolted open as she twisted quickly to face Max who already had his glasses on, ready to go. "You can't go outside. It's the middle of the night. Don't be crazy."

"I have to go outside. I'll go crazy if I stay in here one minute longer. I won't be gone for long." Max started to move aside the loose bale of hay.

"Max, wait," said Gabi, reaching out to block Max's

exit. "Read one of your books or I'll read something to you. Just stay here."

"No one's going to see me. I'll be very quiet. I just need to get outside for a few minutes. Then I'll come back in and go to sleep. Move aside, Gabi, so I can get out."

"No, Max. You can't go!" Gabi was frantic. She felt responsible for Max. And she also knew that Max could put them all in danger by going outside. What if someone saw him? At least he had known enough to wake her first. "Don't you remember the soldiers we saw on the day we arrived? And remember what Mrs. Kos said about staying quiet."

"I don't care about any of that. I just want to go outside," declared Max, stubbornly. "You can't stop me. Don't make a fuss. You'll wake your mother. That would cause a real scene." The children looked over at Mama, breathing deeply in the hay. Max was right. Gabi wasn't about to wake Mama and she wasn't going to abandon Max. There was only one thing to do.

"Wait," Gabi insisted, as Max bent his head to crawl through the tunnel. She took a deep breath. "I'm coming with you." This was madness, but she couldn't let Max leave by himself. Max grinned and nodded as the two of them crept through the opening in the hay. This was what he had wanted. He knew Gabi would come with him, if he woke her up.

Gabi and Max moved quickly and quietly down the ladder into the barn. The cows shifted slightly, swishing their tails, but remained quiet. The fat yellow cat that always greeted Gabi opened one sleepy eye, before dropping its head back into the hay. How clever you are to sleep through this, thought Gabi, as she followed Max out the barn door and into the cold night air. Silently, Max jumped up and down gleefully. Gabi stared anxiously into the night, peering from side to side for any signs of soldiers. It was good to be outside, Gabi had to admit. But she could hardly allow herself to enjoy the fresh air. She was too afraid. So, she stood quietly in the small yard, her back pressed up against the barn door and watched as Max ran back and forth in the fenced-in space.

"Alright, Max," Gabi whispered, minutes later. "That's enough. Let's go back inside." Gabi motioned Max to follow her into the barn. But Max paid no attention. He had other ideas.

"Come on, Gabi. Let's go into the woods. Let's go for a real walk." Max moved toward the end of the yard, unlatching the gate.

"Max, stop!" ordered Gabi, trying to keep her voice at a whisper. Again, Max ignored her. He was already past the gate and walking on the village road that led to a narrow path into the forest. Gabi had no choice but to follow him. Stumbling in the deep snow, Gabi plowed forward to catch up with her cousin. She grabbed him by the arm and swung him around to face her.

"What is the matter with you?" she demanded. "Have you completely lost your mind? We aren't allowed to be out here. We have to go back."

Max stared back at her, his eyes glinting in the moonlight. "Gabi, isn't it great to be free outside the gate? Stop worrying. No one's going to see us."

Gabi sighed, defeated. She wasn't going to convince Max to return to the safety of the barn. And perhaps he was right. It was dark and quiet. What harm would there be in taking a short walk? She suddenly felt the thrill of being outside.

"Okay, Max. But just a few minutes. When I say it's time, promise me you'll go back."

Max nodded and the two of them continued on the path leading into the woods. Gabi was still worried, but determined not to let Max out of her sight. Even among the dense trees, the brightness of the white snow under their feet, mixed with the glow of the moon and stars above, cast just enough light for the two young people to follow the path. The night air was refreshing and even though it was bitterly cold outside, Gabi soon felt a trickle of sweat work its way down the center of her back. Her body felt weak from lack of exercise. She hadn't moved her young legs like this in a long time. And now, they burned with the effort of walking swiftly. But still, for the first time in a long time, she felt glad to be alive.

Further and deeper into the woods they walked, dodging bushes and jumping over downed logs. Before them lay a dark unknown that felt strangely inviting, as if the freedom Gabi longed for was somewhere up ahead. Behind them was the Kos farm and the safety of the barn. Gabi prayed that Mama would continue sleeping. If her mother awoke and discovered they were gone, she would be frantic. It was the thought of Mama that finally prompted Gabi to pull Max by the arm and turn him around to face her. By now, they had been walking for about fifteen minutes, following the path deep into the woods.

"Okay, Max," she said, puffing heavily. She felt hot from walking so fast, but cold from fear. "That's enough. It's time to go back. You promised you'd turn around when I said so."

"Quiet!" whispered Max. "Listen to that noise."

Gabi listened intently for a moment. Mixed with the noise of her own breathing, she heard the sound of a faint blast, followed by the roar of a motor.

"It's coming from over that ridge," said Max, moving off the path toward the noise.

"No!" whispered Gabi, grabbing Max harshly. "We have to go back, now."

Max pulled free. "Come on, Gabi. Let's just see what it is. I promise, after we take a look, I'll go back with you."

Max was already moving ahead and Gabi had to follow. Together, she and Max moved toward the hill, slower this time, pausing periodically to listen for sounds. Now she could hear men's voices intermingled with banging and occasional blasts. The voices were unmistakably German. Quickly, Gabi pulled Max to the ground as they crawled closer to the ridge of the hill and looked over the top.

Chapter Ten

THE ROAD

BELOW, dozens of men were at work, clearing the forest and building the road that Gabi and Max had been told about. From their clothing, Gabi recognized the workers as villagers. These were the local farmers that Father Lensky had said were being forced to work on the road. Large bulldozers plowed through the woods, following the laborers who were planting dynamite to blast away the tree stumps and boulders. Behind the machines, other villagers were digging with shovels, moving rocks, smoothing out the gravel road that was planned for the additional Nazi troops who were to arrive in the future. The clearing was lit up with giant lanterns and huge bonfires. Uniformed soldiers were everywhere, patrolling the area, guarding the villagers at work. Most were armed with rifles. Others held angry dogs on leashes. The farmers looked weary as they worked silently under the glaring eyes of the guards. They kept their distance from the dogs that snarled each time a worker moved closer to the forest.

Gabi covered her ears as another blast exploded through the air, followed by the command to move in and continue clearing. She glanced over at Max. His eyes bulged and his breathing was quick and shallow. On his face was a combination of excitement and dread. As they watched, several of the guard dogs turned and pulled on their leashes, curling their lips in a deep throaty growl.

A Nazi soldier turned to one of the workers who had stopped momentarily to lean on his shovel. "You there," he shouted harshly in German. "We'll tell you when it's time for a break. Get back to work."

Gabi understood what the soldier was saying. She and Max had studied German in school. She watched as the farmer, worn out from the strenuous labor, quickly obeyed the command to return to his task. Meanwhile, the Nazi soldier tossed the dog a chunk of raw steak. The dog pounced on the meat, tearing it apart with enthusiasm. Another soldier smiled. "They can't resist the taste of fresh meat." The two soldiers laughed and continued to inspect the construction.

Gabi and Max ducked their heads. If they were released, the dogs could easily give them away, not to mention tear them apart. Mesmerized, the children had been watching from their hidden place on the ridge for at least ten minutes, and Gabi knew it was time to get out of there. She motioned Max to crawl behind her, back in the direction of the farmhouse. This time, Max didn't argue. The two of them slithered along the ground, until they felt it was safe to stand again. And then they ran on the path, flying through the woods without looking back, tearing past the trees and bushes with only one thought — to get back to the safety of the barn as quickly as possible.

As they ran, Gabi suddenly heard a thud behind her and glanced backward to see Max sprawled in the snow, face down.

"Max, are you alright?" Gabi flung herself down beside her young cousin and tugged on his sleeve. Max nodded. "Come on. Get up. We must keep going." Gabi was panting and pulling hard to help Max off the ground.

"Wait, Gabi. There's something here." Max dug through the soft snow, pulling and wrenching something that protruded from the ground.

"Leave it. Just get up." Gabi continued to tug on Max's arm.

"Just one more second. There, I've got it." Max freed the object from the earth, shoved it into his pocket, and continued to run after Gabi.

The two children didn't stop until they reached the row of farmhouses in the village. Quickly opening the gate, Gabi and Max slipped across the yard, quietly unlatched the barn door, walked past the animals, and crept back up the ladder to the hayloft. Max silently moved aside the loose bale of hay. Gabi dove through the crawl space back into their hiding place, all the while praying that she would find Mama fast asleep.

And sure enough, there was her mother, still snoring softly. She was in the same position as when the children had left. Gabi silently gave thanks that her mother was such a sound sleeper. With Max safely inside the hiding place, Gabi replaced the bale of hay and collapsed on the floor, heaving a giant sigh of relief.

Max crawled up beside her and nudged her silently. "Look," he whispered, reaching into his pocket. "Look what I found." Max pulled an old revolver from inside his jacket and held it up for Gabi to see. "This is what I fell over when we were running."

"Max, throw that thing away." Once again, she glanced over at Mama.

"It can protect us, Gabi." Max's face glowed with excitement. "I'm going to clean it and see if it works. That way, when we go out the next time, I'll shoot anyone who comes near us."

Next time? There isn't going to be a next time, thought Gabi. They were lucky to have made it back safely this time. But, Gabi was too tired to argue. She pulled her doll into her arms and rolled over, turning her back on Max.

Chapter Eleven

EVA'S DISCOVERY

OVER THE NEXT FEW WEEKS, Max woke Gabi several times in the middle of the night and each time he managed to convince her to go out on a night walk. Max carried his gun with him as he dodged from tree to tree. Like a spy, he peered carefully around each tree trunk, holding the gun at shoulder level.

"The coast is clear, Gabi," said Max, jumping forward and pointing the gun directly ahead. "You can move safely now."

Gabi stumbled forward, tripping over her long peasant skirt. "Max, stop it," she said, wearily. "The gun doesn't even work." Max had discovered that the firing pin was broken. But this hadn't stopped him from polishing the revolver late at night, when Gabi's mother was fast asleep.

"The Nazis won't know it's broken," insisted Max. He pointed at a bush in the distance, pretending to fire.

"Max, this isn't a game." But it was no use. To eleven-year-old Max, it was a game — a game that helped him deal with the reality of his life. He wished he could fight the evil Nazis who had taken away his family.

Gabi shuddered and pulled her jacket tighter around her neck. Even though spring was approaching, here in the mountains there was no sign of winter ending. The snow, especially in the woods, was still deep and the air was cold and damp. Nevertheless, it was good to be outdoors.

During their walks, the children made their way to the road, curious to inspect the progress the Nazis were making. They followed the path into the forest, then crept on their stomachs up the last hill, as close to the Nazi camp as they safely could, peering over the top. Keeping a wary eye on the guards and their dogs, they watched the workers dig the trenches and listened to the voices of the patrolling soldiers.

"Maybe we should tell Mama and Mr. Kos what we're seeing in the woods," said Gabi, as she and Max walked swiftly back to the barn one night.

"No!" replied Max, forcefully. "Your mother would be very angry, if she knew what we were doing. And we'd never be allowed outside again. Is that what you want?"

"No," said Gabi, wearily. "Of course not. But there's so much information we're hearing from the Nazis. We should be telling someone about it."

From their hiding place on the hill overlooking the road, Gabi and Max listened to the Nazis talk freely about the building of the road and their grand plans to crush the Russian Red Army. On several visits to the road, Gabi noticed that the Nazi guards had been joined by soldiers from the Hlinka army. She recognized their uniforms from her first day in the village when she and Max had met them walking to the Kos farmhouse. The Nazi guards and the

Hlinka soldiers mingled easily on the road, boasting about their strength and skill and exchanging bits of information. Gabi didn't understand everything she heard, but she understood enough to know how important the information was.

"Forget about it, Gabi," said Max.

"But what about the workers on the road? They're being controlled by the Nazis — like prisoners. Shouldn't we tell someone about that?" Gabi felt increasingly anxious keeping all this to herself.

"We can't tell anyone," Max continued defiantly. "At least, not yet."

"The strange thing is, it doesn't look like the Nazis are making much progress on the road," continued Gabi.

"I know what you mean," said Max. "Sometimes it looks as though they're working on the same part of the road, over and over again."

As they reached the farmhouse, Gabi still felt uneasy. She was disturbed by the risks they were taking during their night walks. Still, she always went with Max when he woke her in the middle of the night. And she had to admit that she enjoyed the adventure of it, exciting and dangerous all at the same time. She knew what they were doing was dangerous and still she wanted to go out. She tried to convince herself that she did the night walks because of Max — to watch out for him and to protect him. But each time, Gabi herself felt eager to venture outside into the dark night.

In fact, their night patrols were making the daytime hours easier. Gabi and Max were so exhausted after their outings that they slept soundly for most of the next day. The day passed quickly and, before they knew it, it was evening and Mr. Kos would call them out of their hiding place. Mama always assumed it was boredom that drained the children of energy and made them nap.

"I'm so glad that the two of you are able to sleep so well during the day," she said one evening, as they sat with the Kos family having soup and bread. "I can't seem to relax during the day. I'm always so worried that soldiers might be passing by the barn. I watch the two of you fast asleep and I'm envious. But at least I sleep well at night."

Max and Gabi exchanged glances. Gabi's great fear was that Mama was going to wake up one night and find the children gone. After each outing, it was a huge relief to discover Mama sleeping peacefully in the hayloft, unaware of their absence.

Gabi rose from the table and began to clear the dishes. Eva followed, balancing the soup pot against her hip. As Gabi piled the plates into the sink, Eva moved closer and whispered in her ear, "I saw you and Max go out last night."

Gabi froze and then spun around to face Eva, breathing unevenly.

"Don't worry," Eva continued, quietly. "I didn't tell anyone."

Gabi glanced over at her mother, still seated at the table. She and Mr. Kos were engaged in their usual animated conversation about the progress of the war. Through the radio that Mr. Kos kept in this kitchen, they had heard the latest report: "March 19, 1944 — Germany occupies Hungary, sending thousands of Jews to concentration camps." Mr. Kos reassured Mama that the Nazis were going to be stopped, while Mama continued to worry about the fate of her missing friends and family members.

Eva motioned Gabi to follow her into the barn, away from the adults. Max trailed behind, curious about what was happening. Past the hanging curtain and inside the barn, Eva turned to face Gabi and Max.

"I was asleep last night when I heard the barn door open. I thought maybe the wind had blown it open and the cows were going to get outside. So, I got up to close it and saw you and Max going into the yard. I watched you go out the gate."

No one replied. Gabi and Max only stared back at Eva.

"Where did you go?" she asked.

"Just to get some air," Gabi said, looking away.

Eva eyed Gabi evenly. "I don't believe you. You were gone too long. Tell me where you went."

"We found the place where the Nazis are building their road," blurted Max. "It's through the woods and up the hill."

"Max, stop," said Gabi, twirling to face her cousin.

"No. Let him talk," said Eva. "I said I didn't tell anyone and I won't."

Gabi glared at Max and then stared back at Eva. "Now that you know this, what are you going to do?" asked Gabi, anxiously.

Eva paused and then replied. "I promise to keep it a secret." Gabi let out a deep breath. "But there's one condition. You have to take me with you the next time you go."

Gabi shook her head. "I ... I don't know," she said. "I'm not even sure we're going to go out again."

Max interrupted. "You know we will, Gabi. We have to see what's happening with the road. Let Eva come with us." He liked Eva.

Gabi took another deep breath and turned to face Eva. "If we say yes, then you have to swear you won't say a word to your grandparents or to anyone else you know."

"I haven't said a word to anyone about you hiding here. And I'm not going to say a word about this. Don't you know you can trust me?"

Gabi hesitated. She still had trouble trusting Eva as a friend. But now Gabi really had no choice. She reached out to take Eva's hand and placed Max's hand on top of theirs. The three young people stood in the barn and shook hands solemnly, agreeing to a new plan.

Chapter Twelve

THE CONVERSATION

IT RAINED FOR THE NEXT TWO WEEKS, a strong, persistent spring downpour that began to wash the snow from the mountaintops and clear the woods of the signs of winter. The rain also dampened any possibility of the three children going outside at night. How would they explain their wet clothing to Mama or to Mr. and Mrs. Kos? And so Gabi and Max waited through more long, boring days and damp, cool nights for a break in the weather and the chance to go outside again.

"It's never going to stop raining," said Max, one dreary evening as he peered outside through the barn boards. A fine misty spray seeped in through the cracks in the panels, leaving a damp film over the straw floor and the walls of the hiding space.

"Max, how many times have I told you to whisper," replied Gabi, as she slapped at a beetle crawling across her leg. Up above her head, she watched a spider spinning a complicated web in a corner bale of hay. Round and round, it wove its sticky, silken threads into ever expanding circles. The barn crawled with bugs. Gabi's body itched from the bug bites she had sustained over the past months. She scratched her arm aimlessly, as she frowned at Max.

"I *am* whispering," replied Max, making a face. He paused. "What time is it?"

"It's five minutes later than when you asked me the last time," whispered Gabi in frustration.

"How can it only be five minutes?" asked Max. "It must be at least an hour later."

"Well, it's not, Max. So stop asking."

"But I'm going crazy in here," said Max, as he flopped back into the hay.

"Well, I will go crazy if you keep on asking me stupid questions."

The two children glared at each other. Mama opened her eyes wearily and looked in their direction. "Children, you must find something to do. What happened to those wonderful daytime naps the two of you used to have?"

What happened was that we have stopped going out at night, thought Gabi. She too longed for the rain to stop and the opportunity for a night walk.

"Where's Mr. Kos?" Max continued. "It must be time for him to come and get us. What if he has forgotten about us or something bad has happened?"

"Max, darling, Mr. Kos has not forgotten us and nothing has happened."

"But, you don't know that, Auntie Judith. Maybe I should just go into the house and check to make sure."

"Mama, make him be quiet," hissed Gabi.

Mama gave Max a sharp look. "No, Max. You will not

go into the house. We will wait right here. Is that understood?"

Max nodded reluctantly and lay back once more. Minutes passed.

"What time is it now, Gabi?" whispered Max.

"That's it, Mama. I can't take his questions anymore. I'm going into the house to look for Mr. Kos. I have to go to the toilet anyway and I can't wait any longer," she added.

Reluctantly, Mama sighed once more. "Just be careful, Gabi."

Gabi nodded and crawled over to the exit, ignoring Max's dirty look as she passed. She moved the bale of hay aside, scrambled through the tunnel into the barn, and climbed down the ladder.

The Kos farmhouse had no indoor plumbing. Like most houses in the village, the family used an outhouse. To avoid Gabi and her family having to go outside and risk being seen, Mr. Kos had placed a pail by the curtain that separated the house from the barn. When darkness fell each night, Mr. Kos emptied the pail and replaced it. Sometimes Gabi felt she would rather explode than use the pail. There was no privacy and it smelled.

Gabi plugged her nose while she finished and stood up to straighten her skirt. She could just make out the sounds of conversation coming from inside the house. Maybe Mr. Kos had forgotten them after all, she thought as she moved the curtain aside and stepped into the hallway. She tiptoed down the passage, creeping forward until she stood just outside the kitchen area. From there, she could hear Mr. and Mrs. Kos's conversation without being seen.

"I don't like having them here, Stephan. I can't help the way I feel about it."

"Maria, we've been through all of this so many times."

"I know, but I must have been mad to do this. No one — not one of our neighbors — would risk their lives like this. People around here would turn in a Jew for a bowl of soup. And what do we do? We house them and feed them and put ourselves in all kinds of danger."

"Maria, you agreed to have Judith and her family come to stay with us."

"I know I did. But I never expected they would be here this long. I thought maybe a month — two at the most. But it's been almost three months and who knows how much longer it will be. And we never agreed to the boy. When we first made plans to have them come, it was just the woman and her daughter. Having that boy here makes it even more dangerous." Gabi couldn't see Mrs. Kos, but she pictured her nervously clasping and unclasping her hands as she spoke. "The other night, when he was running around the kitchen, I thought I would strangle him. With all the noise he was making, it's a wonder that our neighbors didn't hear him. No matter how many times I tell him to be quiet, he just ignores me."

"He's a boy, Maria. He needs an opportunity to run around. Evenings are the only time he has that chance."

"Well, he's trouble, that much I know. And he's going to get *us* into trouble with his tricks and performances. And the girl — well, she says nothing. She just stares at me. I don't like it, Stephan. I don't like it one bit."

"I like her." At the sound of Eva's voice, Gabi's ears suddenly perked up. "Gabi talks to me."

"What does she say? Does she say things about us?" asked Mrs. Kos. Gabi froze. How was Eva going to answer? Would she tell her grandparents about the night walks?

There was a moment of silence and then Eva began to speak again. "Gabi talks about things she used to do before the war. She misses her friends, grandma. Most of them were arrested and taken away by the soldiers. A few of the lucky ones escaped. But she doesn't even know what's become of them. Gabi knows it's dangerous to be here. And she's scared just as you are."

"You see, Maria," continued Mr. Kos, "they're all scared. And I know you're frightened too. But what would you have us do? Do you want to turn them over to the authorities? Is that what you want?"

Gabi strained to hear the answer. It was several seconds before Mrs. Kos finally replied. "No. Of course that's not what I want. I just want it all to go away — the war, the fear, and the hiding."

"It's what we all want, Maria," said Mr. Kos. "But for now it continues." Gabi pictured Mr. Kos stroking his wife's arm, reassuringly. "And we will continue to do the right thing."

"I suppose," said Mrs. Kos. "But Evichka, I don't want you talking to that girl. I don't want you to become friends with her."

"She's nice, grandma, and she is my friend. I even think

she is beginning to trust me."

"Don't worry about it so much, Maria," said Mr. Kos. "It's good for the girls to have each other."

Gabi had heard enough. Silently, she turned and walked quickly down the hallway, back into the barn and up into the hayloft. She paused outside the tunnel, thinking about what she had just heard. Mrs. Kos's reluctance to have them hiding in her barn came as no surprise to Gabi. Thank goodness Mr. Kos was there to reassure his wife, Gabi thought. What surprised her was Eva. In spite of Eva's intrusive behavior, she did seem to think of Gabi as her friend. Here in the misery of her hiding place, Gabi desperately wanted and needed a friend. Somehow she felt better about the thought of Eva coming with her and Max on a night walk.

Once again, Gabi prayed for the rain to stop. She pushed aside the bale of hay and bent her head to crawl through the tunnel. If we don't get outside soon, I'll strangle Max before Mrs. Kos does, thought Gabi. Then, she heard the sound of Mr. Kos calling to her family to come into the house for something to eat.

Chapter Thirteen
THE TRIO

THE OPPORTUNITY FOR a night walk finally came two weeks later. The day began like any other. Gabi, Mama, and Max awoke around noon and spent the rest of the day resting, reading, and playing word games. It felt warmer that day, as if spring had finally reached the mountain village. In the late afternoon, Max crawled over to where Gabi lay in the hayloft. Glancing cautiously back at Mama, he mouthed to her, "Tonight, Gabi. I want to go out tonight. What do you think?"

Gabi looked over his shoulder at Mama who was resting in the corner of their hiding place. She took a deep breath and nodded at Max. Later that evening, while the two girls were clearing the table of dishes, she had the chance to speak to Eva.

"If you're going to come with us, then tonight's the night," whispered Gabi.

Eva's face brightened and she nodded enthusiastically. "Yes," she replied. "I'll come to the yard after my grandparents are asleep and meet you there. Wait for me."

Gabi didn't sleep at all that night. And she knew from

the movement next to her that Max wasn't sleeping either. Silently, the children waited with anticipation for Mama's breathing to become deep and even. Even then, they waited until the darkest part of the night. Then they rose together and moved through the hay tunnel, down the barn ladder, past the sleeping animals, and into the yard.

"I'm over here," a voice called from the corner of the house. Eva moved out from the shadows to join Gabi and Max. "I couldn't sleep, so I've been waiting for you." Gabi and Max nodded. "I brought this for you, Gabi." Eva reached around her and pulled out a pair of heavy woolen overalls. "You can't go roaming in the woods dressed like that." She pointed to Gabi's long peasant skirt.

Gabi reached out to take the clothes and then moved behind the barn to change, grateful for Eva's thoughtfulness. The overalls would make trekking through the woods so much easier. When she emerged several minutes later, Eva nodded with approval at her appearance.

"Well, what are we waiting for?" said Eva. "Let's go."

"Wait," said Gabi, feeling responsible. "Let's be clear about a few things. First of all, when I say it's time to go back, we go. Understand? No discussion and no arguments." Eva nodded. "Secondly, we don't take any chances. We must stay together and we must be careful." Gabi was still nervous about having Eva along.

"I understand, Gabi," said Eva. "Don't worry. I won't do anything stupid."

"It's this way, Eva. Follow me." Ignoring Gabi's stern warning, Max took off through the gate, pulling Eva behind him. Gabi followed, whispering in the night air for Max to stay close and not get too far ahead.

Through the woods they moved, Max in front, directing the way, followed by Eva and Gabi, who continued to glance behind for any sign of trouble. Several times, the children dove for the cover of trees and fallen stumps when they thought they heard unfamiliar noises. They waited in silent anticipation. Max kept his gun out, pointed into the darkness as if he really would be able to protect them in the event of real danger. But each time the noise passed and the children eventually resumed their walk. It's probably a fox or some other night animal out prowling just like we are, thought Gabi. Their night walks were becoming strangely familiar and comfortable.

Finally, sounds of the laborers working on the road began to reach them. Gabi motioned for Max and Eva to crouch down as they approached the final ridge and peered over the hill at the road. In the past few weeks, the road construction had not progressed with any great speed. Yet the Nazis seemed intent on working through the night to complete the road. Gabi, Max, and Eva looked on silently as the workers pounded the ground with their spades, digging steadily in a drum-like beat. Soldiers and guard dogs stood nearby, patrolling the perimeter of the construction site. Gabi tapped Eva on the shoulder and silently motioned toward the guards. Eva nodded and instinctively lowered her head.

After some time, Gabi signaled to Max and Eva that it was time to leave. The three children backed away from their observation hill and crawled to safety some distance away. Then, they began to run, not looking back for a moment. Finally, Gabi raised her hand to indicate that they could stop running. Now Eva took over, leading them to a clearing, deep in the forest. Here the three children fell onto the ground, breathing heavily.

"That was incredible," said Eva. "Did you see all the soldiers? I counted about twenty of them, and maybe fifty or sixty workers. I recognized some of the men from my village. But the others must be from other villages around here." Eva paused to catch her breath. "My grandparents would never let me come out here."

Gabi raised herself on one arm and looked over at Eva. "Remember, you promised you'd keep all of this a secret."

"Why do you sometimes act as though you don't trust me?" asked Eva.

How could Gabi explain how hard it was for her to trust anyone these days. "I don't know," she began. "You ask so many questions."

Eva sighed. "I'm trying to understand what's happening all around us — why there's a war, why you have to hide, why being Jewish matters so much. My grandfather says no one deserves to be treated like the Jews are being treated. I stare at you because I can't imagine being in your shoes, hiding the way you have to hide. Don't you understand, Gabi? I think you're so brave."

Gabi floundered. Eva's boldness was actually admiration.

"What about me?" interrupted Max. "Don't you think

I'm brave too?"

Eva smiled and reached over to ruffle Max's hair. "Oh, you're the bravest one of all," she said. "You led the way. We wouldn't be out here if it weren't for you." Eva turned back to face Gabi. "So, can you stop worrying now? I'd never tell anyone about this. Besides, if I said anything, then I wouldn't be able to come back with you."

"It's like we're spies," said Max. "We can watch the building of the road and look out for trouble. And I can shoot anyone who gets in our way." He waved his gun dramatically.

Gabi ignored her cousin and glanced around. "Where are we, Eva?" Eva had lead them to a small opening deep in the forest. A few fallen logs lay scattered on the ground and one large tree stump stood like a throne in the center of the clearing. A thick forest wall surrounded the area.

"I come here in the summertime with my grandfather," said Eva. "He sits on that tree stump and tells me stories about what it was like on the farm when he was a young boy. This is our secret place. No one knows about it and my grandmother can never find us here." Eva smiled. "She means well, but sometimes I need a break from her."

Gabi nodded. "What do you think will happen when the road is finished?"

"I guess more Nazi soldiers will come up here," said Eva. "I heard on my grandfather's radio that the Russians are moving closer to us from the east. They've already taken back parts of the Ukraine and Poland that were captured by the Nazis earlier in the war. My grandfather says the Nazis are scared. They need to bring more troops into this area to defend themselves."

"If there were a big battle here," said Max with growing excitement, "we could be a part of it."

"Stop it, Max," said Gabi, annoyed. "We're not going to be in any battle. But if we don't get back to the barn, we're going to have a big battle with Mama." She started to rise from the ground and then froze at the new sounds of movement in the forest.

"What was that?" Gabi heard a noise from behind the trees.

"Oh, probably just another fox or rabbit," said Max, confidently.

A branch broke off behind the children, while up ahead came the swishing noise of several people moving through the woods.

"Max, Eva, get up. Run!" screamed Gabi, as several men, armed with rifles, broke through the trees to surround the children.

Chapter Fourteen

THE PARTISANS

GABI'S HEART POUNDED with a fear she had not known for some time. All she could think was that the Nazis had found them and that they were going to be sent to a concentration camp like Magda. Gabi wanted to run, but there was no way out. She quickly counted four, five, six soldiers.

"Who are you? What are you doing here?" a soldier shouted, as his comrades moved closer to surround the children.

Eva was breathing heavily beside Gabi, when suddenly Max made a break for it. He ran directly toward the soldiers, trying to push through their line, desperate to escape. Gabi screamed as two soldiers reached down to grab Max. They picked him up easily and held him above the ground, his legs dangling below him.

"Whoa, young soldier. Just where do you think you are going?" One of the men tapped Max with his gun as Max struggled to be released.

Fearing for her cousin, Gabi cried, "Put him down! Don't hurt him." She turned to face the soldier who had ordered them to stop and for the first time looked closely at his uniform. There was something strange about his clothing. He wore an unrecognizable army jacket, high workboots, and a dark cap pulled down to cover his ears. He looked unshaven and messy. She glanced over at the other soldiers. Each one was dressed in a different uniform. One of the soldiers holding Max looked just a bit older than Gabi, while the one giving orders was close to thirty. A couple of the soldiers were women, also in uniforms and carrying guns.

"You're not Nazis?" Gabi asked.

The soldier in charge laughed. "No. We're partisans, mostly Slovaks. But in our brigade, we also have soldiers from Hungary and Poland. You can be sure there are no Nazis. My name is Vladimir. My name means to rule with greatness and I am the commander of this troop. Set the boy down," he ordered the soldiers who held Max.

The soldiers lowered Max to the ground. Max rushed over to Gabi and threw his arms around her neck, as Eva moved closer as well. Gabi held Max with one arm and Eva with the other. The three children huddled together protectively as Gabi's mind raced back over what she knew about the partisans. Joseph and Mr. Kos had talked about the partisans. They were soldiers, men and women who lived in the forest in makeshift camps and caves, and attacked Nazi forces whenever they could.

"Now, who are you and where are you from?" asked Vladimir.

"I'm from the village back there," replied Eva.

"That's right," Gabi shot a look at Eva. "We're all from the village." Gabi didn't want Eva to say too much. Who were these partisans? And how did they feel about Jews? The commander seemed friendly enough, but Gabi still didn't feel safe. Instinctively, she moved even closer to Max.

"What are you doing out here in the middle of the night?" Vladimir asked. Max described the night walks in the forest to watch the progress of the Nazi road. The commander listened attentively.

"Yes, we know about the road. We've also been watching. Last month, one of our units blew up a portion of the railway tracks on which trains brought building supplies to this area from Germany. The Nazis think they're gaining headway with their road and then — boom — we give them a little surprise to slow them down. That's our job, to stop them wherever and whenever we can." Vladimir smiled cunningly, as the soldiers around him laughed and nodded.

Suddenly, Gabi understood why the Nazis never seemed to be making progress on the road. Every time the soldiers completed a few feet of new road, the partisans moved in to destroy it. She looked at their captors with increased interest and admiration.

"Where do you get your guns?" asked Max, eyeing their rifles.

"We steal them," Vladimir replied. "We steal guns, we steal food and whatever else we can. Sometimes the townspeople are good to us. They feed us or give us shelter. But most of the time we're on our own, using our wits to get by."

"Now I recognize you," said Eva to Vladimir. "You came by our farmhouse some time ago and my grandparents gave you food."

Vladimir nodded. "Some people help us and some don't. We must always be careful and look out for ourselves."

That's just like us, thought Gabi.

"I have a gun. I found it." Max pulled the revolver from his pocket and showed it to Vladimir who whistled in appreciation.

"So, you're a young soldier, are you? Have you fired it?"

Max shook his head. "No," he said. "It doesn't work, but you didn't know that, did you?"

"Do you want to be a partisan, young man?" asked Vladimir. "Do you want to be a soldier who fights the enemy?"

Max nodded eagerly. "Yes, of course. I want to be a soldier and protect my family."

"Well, maybe you can be of some help to us. We need scouts who will watch the movement of the Nazis in this area. You can report to us if you see anything unusual or anything you think we need to know. Would you do that?"

Max's eyes behind his glasses nearly burst from their sockets. He looked at Gabi and Eva, and back at Vladimir. "Oh, yes sir!" he shouted. "We can go out at night and spy on the Nazis. We'll let you know if we see anything!"

"Good," said Vladimir, nodding with approval. "If you bring us information and perhaps some food, we might let you work with us. And now, my young soldiers, we need to return to our campsite and you had better get back to your farm."

As they said good-by to the partisan soldiers, Gabi couldn't help but feel excited. This was just the opportunity she needed. She wanted to talk to adults about what the Nazis were doing. She wanted to share their information with people who might be able to use it against the Nazis. She loved the feeling that she could do something useful, rather than just hiding in the barn. The children said little as they quickly ran back to the house. But when they reached the gate, they stopped and faced one another.

"We're going back to the forest soon, right?" said Max. Gabi nodded. This time she didn't need convincing.

"And I'm coming with you," said Eva.

Chapter Fifteen

LIFE IN THE FOREST

A WEEK LATER, Gabi, Max, and Eva returned to the forest to look for the partisans. At first, the children weren't quite sure how to find the soldiers. So they did the only thing they could think of. They crept back to the hill above the road. Gabi noticed that there now seemed to be more guards on patrol. After watching the road for a few minutes, Eva led Gabi and Max to the same spot where, a week earlier, the partisans had discovered them. There they sat down and waited.

They didn't need to wait long. Soon, they heard rustling in the trees behind them. A group of partisan soldiers emerged from the forest, led by the same commander, Vladimir. Once again, the small band surrounded the children.

"Well, well, if it isn't our young scouts," said Vladimir in a friendly tone.

Gabi cleared her throat. "We want to help," she said, nervously. "We want to tell you about the things we've seen on the road."

"We want to be soldiers like you," said Max.

The partisan commander looked at the children for a moment. "So you think you can give us important information?" Gabi, Max, and Eva nodded. "Well, perhaps you'd like to see our campsite. We can sit together and you can tell us what you know." The children looked at each other and then at the partisan soldier, nodding their heads in reply.

Vladimir turned on his heel and began to walk swiftly into the woods. The other soldiers motioned for Gabi, Max, and Eva to follow. Out of the clearing, deeper and deeper into the forest, they walked in single file. Turning this way and that, it felt to Gabi as if they were walking in circles. By the time the group emerged into a new clearing, she had no idea where they were. Even Eva, who had spent her life exploring these woods, was confused.

Gabi looked around, curiously. Throughout the clearing, there were dozens of tent-shaped structures made of branches, tied together to provide shelter, and covered with dingy gray blankets. More blankets and straw mattresses were scattered on the ground, along with pots and other cooking gear. At the center of the clearing, a soldier tended a large fire pit, ladling some kind of steaming liquid into tin cups that were being passed to others. Smaller fires were being tended by soldiers throughout the campsite. There was a wagon in one corner of the camp, piled with food supplies and covered ammunition. The campsite buzzed with activity.

Gabi counted eighty or ninety soldiers altogether. Some soldiers were eating, some were washing clothing, some were counting ammunition, and some were just lying on the ground resting. She noted with interest how different they looked from each other. There were soldiers who were old and ragged looking with deep lines etched on their worn faces. And there were young boys, only a few years older than Gabi, boys with clean, unshaven faces and eager, enthusiastic eyes. There were young women who moved easily among the men, exchanging conversation and sharing food. There were soldiers wearing Slovak uniforms, as well as those dressed in the army uniforms of Hungary, Poland, and Romania. Their outfits were scruffy and unkempt. It was hard to imagine that these tattered looking men and women were really soldiers.

Vladimir yelled to one of the young men. "Dominik, it's your turn to stand watch. Go relieve Kornel from his guard duties."

The young soldier jumped up, as he heard his name called. Gabi recognized him from the forest. He was one of the soldiers who had grabbed Max when he tried to escape. Dominik nodded at her. He was a fair haired, serious looking young man with piercing brown eyes. "There's always work to do," he said. Then he grabbed a rifle and marched off into the woods.

The commander slung his own rifle off his shoulder, slumped down beside one of the fire pits, and reached over to scoop a cup of hot liquid from one of the pots simmering on the fire. Only then did he turn his attention back to Gabi, Max, and Eva, motioning them to join him on the ground. A young woman sat silently next to the commander, cleaning her pistol, indifferent to the commotion around her.

"Here in the woods we have the advantage," Vladimir said. "We know this area better than the Nazis do. I know every inch of this forest. I know where each swamp is located, where every tree stump sticks out of the forest floor." He gestured around the campsite. "Most of us could travel through the woods with our eyes closed and never stumble. We've settled in well here," he continued, "but our camp is completely moveable. We can pack up and be out of here instantly. And that is something we often do. We stay in one place for a few nights and then move on. Our motto is: 'Sleep in your clothes, guard your weapon with your life, and be prepared to move at a moment's notice.' That way we can't be captured by the enemy." The commander sipped from his cup. "So, my young scouts," he said, "tell me what you have heard and seen in the woods."

The three children told Vladimir how they had begun their night walks weeks earlier. They told him about discovering the road and watching the Nazi soldiers with their guard dogs on patrol. Then they talked about returning to see the progress of the road construction. The partisan leader chuckled when they questioned the lack of progress the Nazis seemed to be making.

"We do our job well, don't we?" said Vladimir. "We have blasted that road with dynamite several times. But that's not all we've done. We've destroyed Nazi telegraph lines, power plants, and factories. We'll do anything we can to stop the Nazis." Vladimir spoke with much determination and pride.

Finally, Gabi, Max, and Eva told Vladimir about Mr.

Kos's radio and the news reports about the German occupation of Hungary.

Vladimir listened and then stopped the children with a wave of his hand. "So far, you've told me things we already know," he said. "If you want to be spies, you'll have to bring me new information."

"Here's something you may want to know," Gabi said, glancing over at Max and Eva. "The Nazis are taking Jews to concentration camps and killing them there."

The partisan commander shrugged. "We've heard those rumors about the work camps."

"These aren't rumors," insisted Gabi. "And they're not work camps. They're death camps." Taking a deep breath, she told Vladimir about the letter from Magda. For the first time, the commander sat forward and listened intently.

"You've heard from someone who has been taken away? You know the Nazis are killing Jews in the camps? How did you get this letter?"

Gabi paused before answering. Telling Vladimir about the letter meant telling him that she and Max were Jews in hiding. Were they ready to disclose this? Max tugged on her arm and nodded. Eva, standing close by, gave her silent consent. And so, Gabi began to speak. She talked about the farmhouse and Mama. She described the hayloft in the barn and how long they had been hiding there. She talked about Eva and Mr. and Mrs. Kos and the risks they were taking. She even talked about Father Lensky and Joseph. The partisan leader stopped Gabi periodically to ask a question or to clarify a point. Finally, he sat back, nodding with satisfaction.

"That's good, my young friends," he said. "You've brought me good information. So, I've already told you my name. Now, tell me your names." The children shook hands with Vladimir and responded with their own names.

"Are there other partisan bands like this one?" asked Max.

Vladimir nodded. "Oh yes. There are at least thirty brigades scattered throughout this region — groups of soldiers each led by a different commander. Many of the units are bigger than we are. Together, we are planning a major assault on the Nazis. It will be soon, sometime this summer. Sabina here is our radio operator." Vladimir indicated the woman next to him. "We are in constant contact with the other units, exchanging information and coordinating our movements. Your information about the concentration camps will be helpful to us. Facts about the Nazi killing camps will help persuade others to join our movement — to resist the Nazis." The woman named Sabina looked up, nodded at the children, and then continued to polish her gun.

"There's something else you should know," said Gabi. "Today, when the three of us went by the road, I noticed that there were more soldiers than ever before. I don't know what that means. But I thought it might be important."

"I'm not sure," said Vladimir, leaning forward with interest. "It could mean that more Nazi soldiers are moving into this area. We'll contact our other units," he continued, nodding to Sabina. "We'll see what they have to say."

"Does that mean we can come back?" asked Max. "We'll bring you even more information next time we come."

"And we'll try to bring you some food, too." Eva spoke up for the first time. "We don't have much. But we'll bring you whatever we can."

Vladimir paused a moment and then nodded. "Yes, my young soldiers, you can return. Bring us food. That is always welcome. And watch the road. If you see anything unusual, report it to me. But I must warn you. If there is trouble or my comrades feel that you are a burden in any way, your visits will have to stop. We won't risk our safety for anyone, even for young scouts with information. Is that clear?"

The children nodded, solemnly. Gabi felt excited. They were helping the partisan soldiers! They were doing something useful and important. In a small way, they were fighting back for all their bad experiences in this war. Suddenly, Gabi felt powerful and strong.

"And now, my young soldiers, you need to leave," said Vladimir, as he stood and glanced up at the sky. "It's almost daylight. Your families will worry."

Daylight! Gabi gasped and looked up as well. Indeed, the light of day was approaching. Not only were they in danger of being seen, but also Mama would be waking up. Even Eva looked scared at the thought of finding her grandparents awake back at the farm. The children had to run fast, if they were going to return to the farm before the sun rose. Vladimir directed them back out of the clearing into the woods from where the children ran toward the village. Out of breath, they reached the gate and opened it.

Moving silently, Gabi, Max, and Eva crept across the yard toward the barn. Max lifted the latch on the barn door and swung it open, careful not to make a creaking sound. As the barn door closed behind them, the three children turned to face Mr. Kos and Mama.

Chapter Sixteen

A DEAL WITH MAMA

"Where have you been?" For the first time, Mr. Kos's voice was sharp. For a moment, no one spoke. The adults stared at the three children, waiting for an explanation. Their faces showed a combination of anger and relief. "Do you have any idea how terrified we have been? Your grandmother is inside, so sick with worry she had to lie down."

Gabi turned to her mother. "Mama, I'm so sorry. We lost track of time. We —"

"Lost track of time? You should be in the hayloft with me — not outside, keeping track of time." Mama was furious.

"I know it was dangerous and stupid. But it's been so hard to stay in the barn day after day, night after night. We just wanted to be outside for a short while." It was useless. Gabi's reasoning was weak. She knew that in Mama's eyes there would be no excuse for taking this kind of risk.

"It was my fault," Eva suddenly spoke up. "I convinced Gabi and Max to go out at night and take me with them."

Mr. Kos turned to face his granddaughter. "Evichka, how could you do this?" he asked harshly. "You know how dangerous it is for us to hide Gabi and her family. We've trusted you with all the information about what we are doing. Now you've put us all at risk. I don't know how we can trust you again."

"No," said Gabi. She couldn't allow Eva to take the blame for what she and Max had been doing for some time. "It's not Eva's fault." Gabi avoided her mother's eyes as she began to explain about the night walks that she and Max had been taking. "We thought we would do it only once. I knew it was wrong, but it was a kind of adventure. And it felt so good to be outside. After we discovered the road, we just needed to go again and again," she added, looking directly at Mr. Kos. "But tonight, Mama, we met the partisans in the forest. They've been camping there for some time, destroying parts of the road."

"There are hundreds of them in the forest, Auntie Judith. They're on our side. They're fighting against the Nazis. And they want us to help them." Max explained how the partisan commander had invited the children to continue their night patrols and report anything unusual about the building of the road. Mama looked horrified.

"This is madness!" she wailed, looking to Mr. Kos for support and then back to the children. "It's a miracle that you haven't been caught by the Nazis until now. I forbid you to go out again."

Mr. Kos thought for a moment. "I know about these partisans. The work they are doing to help overthrow the Nazis is dangerous, but also important. If there is some way the children can help, maybe we should let them do it. Gabi and Max are clever. Look what they've managed to do already — even under our watchful eyes. And Evichka has known her way around these forests since she was an infant."

"Yes, Mama. It feels like we're doing something to help, instead of just sitting around hiding and waiting. Please say you'll let us go." Gabi pleaded with her mother.

It was unusual for Gabi to disagree with Mama. She hardly recognized herself, arguing defiantly like this. But something had overcome her there in the forest — a new sense of strength and freedom. How could she explain to her mother what it felt like to be with the partisans?

Gabi had been eight years old when the war broke out in 1939. For years, other people had told her when she could play outside, with whom she could play, when she could shop, and even where she could walk. She had hated it. Now for the first time, she felt in charge of what she was doing. And that felt good, even if her actions were upsetting to Mama. Gabi was determined that somehow she would get her mother to agree to their plan to return to the forest.

Meanwhile, Mama continued to resist. Mr. Kos took the children's side. He suggested he could get false identification papers for Gabi and Max, stating that they were Catholic. Mama argued that, while Gabi might be able to pass for a local with her blond hair, the papers would probably do little good for Max who had dark eyes and dark hair. Mama also voiced her concern that not all partisans were friendly to Jews. How could the partisans be trusted not to turn on the children? Mr. Kos insisted that, whatever their prejudice against Jews, the main goal of the partisans was to defeat the Nazis. When Mr. Kos offered that the children could bring extra food to the partisans, Mama reminded him that he had barely enough food for his own family.

Max watched as the discussion continued. Like Gabi, he felt the need to be with the partisans and do something useful. The partisan commander had called him a young soldier and that's what he wanted to be — a soldier who could fight the enemy that had taken away his family. Surely, Auntie Judith could understand how much that meant to him.

"Last night, there was another report on the radio," continued Mr. Kos. "Two Jewish inmates managed to escape from a concentration camp called Auschwitz. They brought more information about the treatment of Jews, reports that confirm what your cousin Magda wrote to you. Jews are being murdered by the thousands. This is important information for the partisans. It will increase their determination to do everything in their power to stop the Nazis. The children have an important role to play here, Judith. I know it is frightening to think of them returning into the woods. But they have the opportunity to bring this kind of information to the partisans. Can you see how important this might be?"

Mama closed her eyes and gulped. The world was closing in on all Jews in Europe. But at least here, in this barn with her children close to her, she had felt a sense of safety. With the knowledge that Gabi and Max had left the hayloft to go into the woods, this illusion suddenly disappeared. Yet their obvious determination to help the partisans was admirable. She looked over at Gabi and Max and her heart filled with love. How young they were to have to suffer so much in this war. And how brave they were to want to do something to help. She understood their need to take charge, to feel they were fighting back for all the terrible things that had happened to them. But how could she bear to let them go? She, too, needed courage and strength.

Finally, Mama turned to face Gabi. "You are so young and so brave, my darling Gabilinka. Your Papa would be so proud of you." Gabi swallowed hard as Mama reached out to stroke her cheek. "And you too, Max. Your parents and your sister would admire your courage. Maybe, by going out at night, you'll be helping them in some way."

Gabi threw herself into her mother's arms, while Max stood still, blinking back his own tears. He was going to be a soldier and that was most important. Eva moved forward and Mama took her hand as well. "But promise me," she continued, "from now on, you will wake me when you go out at night. If you are going to be out there and take such risks, then at least I have the right to be awake and worry about you!"

Gabi looked up and smiled at her mother. "That's a deal."

Chapter Seventeen

DOMINIK

THE NEXT TIME Gabi, Max, and Eva went to the forest, Mama was awake when they left. This time it seemed as if the partisans were waiting for them in the woods. The children had barely arrived at Eva's secret clearing in the center of the forest when they were surrounded by a patrol of partisan soldiers who again escorted them to their campsite.

Vladimir greeted them. "Ah, my young scouts. Welcome, welcome. It's good to have you back with us." His smile was warm and hospitable, like the host at a social gathering. Gabi was grateful for his lighthearted manner, though she knew the seriousness of this gathering.

"We've brought you something to eat," said Eva, reaching into the bag she had slung over her shoulder. From inside, she pulled out a loaf of bread, some potatoes and onions, a head of cabbage, and a large chunk of strong smelling cheese. "It's not much," she said apologetically, "but it's something."

Eva's grandmother had not been pleased to part with the food. "Now we're going to feed the forest as well as the others," she had said, pointing toward the barn, clenching and unclenching her fists in dismay. As always, her husband reassured her that they were doing the right thing. "Maria, it is our duty to help the partisans. They're trying to end this war. Would you let them go hungry?" His wife did not answer and quickly left the room, muttering under her breath. Mr. Kos had helped Eva pack the supplies that she was now distributing to the partisans.

Gabi talked to Vladimir and told him about the latest radio report from Mr. Kos: the news from the escaped inmates from Auschwitz. Vladimir listened carefully and then turned to talk to Sabina, the radio operator.

"Relay this news to the other units," he said. "Let them know there are more confirming reports about the death camps." He turned back to Gabi and placed his hand on her shoulder, nodding with approval. Then he turned to the food that Eva had brought.

"This is wonderful," bellowed Vladimir, piercing the skin of a potato with his knife and throwing it on the fire to bake. "A real feast. My young scouts are providing us with information and food, both welcome additions." Vladimir motioned to a soldier standing close by. "Dominik," he called. "Come and get the supplies and distribute them to the others."

Gabi remembered the young man from their previous visit to the campsite. "Hello," she said, extending her hand. "You were on guard duty the last time we were here, right?"

Dominik smiled and shook hands with each of the children. "I take care of security and food. I'm not sure which of my jobs is more important. I'll make tea and then we can divide up this food and take it to some of the soldiers in the camp. They'll be grateful for what you've brought." Dominik strode toward the campfire, stoking the flames underneath the pot of water that boiled rapidly in the center. He moved comfortably around the campsite, motioning the three children to stand back as the flames from the fire roared into the sky. The smell of crackling wood filled the air. Dominik added some tea leaves into the pot, stirred, and then poured the mild brew into several cups.

Eva looked at the young man with interest. Dominik towered over most of the other soldiers, even though he looked just a few years older than Eva. He was a young boy and yet here he was, a soldier in a partisan unit, fighting the Nazi enemy. Only his thin body and his deep brown eyes betrayed the hardships of being caught in a war.

"Is there something you want to ask me? You keep staring at me." Dominik looked up from the fire he was tending.

"I'm ... I'm sorry," said Eva, her face flushed with embarrassment. "It's just ... well I am curious ... I mean ... how did you ever get here?"

Dominik looked around. "No one around here asks about a past. We have only one future together and that is to get rid of our enemy. That's what matters."

"I'm sorry," Eva blurted. "It's just that you look so young."

Gabi sat listening to the conversation. She had been on the receiving end of Eva's probing questions in the past. But now she appreciated Eva's keen curiosity. She wanted to know more about Dominik as well.

Dominik snorted. "I'm seventeen, old enough to be a soldier. And if you must know, I've been with this unit for two years."

"But what about your family?" Gabi joined into the conversation, happy that Eva had broken the ice with the young soldier. "How did your parents ever let you join? Aren't they worried about you?"

"My family is dead," said Dominik, matter-of-factly. "Killed by the Nazis in a raid of our village several years ago. My mother was a Jew. My Christian father tried to hide all of us in a cave up in the mountains close to our home, along with other Jews. But a unit of the local Hlinka found out about our hiding place. They raided the cave early one morning, while we were all sleeping. Only a few of us managed to escape. My parents and most of the others were not so lucky." Dominik hung his head and was silent for a moment.

Then he looked up, his eyes narrow and defiant. "I made my way into the forest and linked up with this partisan unit. They didn't know my age, only that I was strong and determined. I cooked their meals, cleaned their clothes and weapons, and delivered messages to other units. Vladimir taught me how to shoot a gun and took me along on a raid to blow up the railway tracks. I've been fighting with the partisans ever since. And I'm going to keep fighting — until every Nazi is dead."

There was pain in Dominik's eyes, even as he fought to conceal it. The war had robbed him of so much — his family, his home, his life as a normal teenager. Now, Dominik lived only for justice, avenging the death of his parents.

I'm so much like him, marveled Max as he listened to Dominik's story and thought again about his own family. My parents are gone, just like Dominik's, and I also want to do something to get back at the enemy. Max stared admiringly at Dominik, in awe of his courage and determination.

Dominik smiled at Max. "Here," he said. "Why don't you bring some tea to the other soldiers." Max jumped up. He wanted to be the first to help. He picked up a cup of tea, looked around, and walked toward a man sitting alone by another fire pit. "Excuse me," said Max, "would you like some tea?"

At first, there was no answer. The man was slumped over, his head down. As Max moved closer, he noticed that the soldier looked older than the other men in the camp. His uniform was torn in several places and ragged, as if he didn't care about his appearance. The man continued to sit silently as Max repeated his question, this time louder. "I said, would you like something to drink?"

"I heard you the first time," the man answered without raising his head. "Do you think I'm deaf? And do you think I'd take anything from a Jewish troublemaker? Get away from me."

Max froze and shuddered. The soldier's words pierced through him like sharp needles. Max recognized the sound of hatred in his voice. He had heard it before on the streets of his own village. The soldier threw back his head and laughed a long sinister cackle. Max could see his wild angry eyes. "That got your attention, didn't it? Jewish troublemaker! I'd get a nice reward if I turned you over to the Nazis. Now get lost!"

Max turned blindly and stumbled away. He could hear the soldier snickering behind his back, laughing at Max as he staggered back to Gabi and Eva.

"What's the matter?" asked Eva with concern, as Max collapsed next to the fire. "You look like you're going to be sick."

Max felt humiliated and scared. All his bravado had left him and he was weak with fear. With Dominik listening, he told Eva and Gabi what the soldier had said. Dominik shrugged when Max got to the part about the soldier threatening to turn him over to the Nazis.

"Can he do that? Can he turn us in?" asked Max, still trembling.

"Don't mind Erik," said Dominik. "He would never turn you in because, if he did, he would be caught as well."

"You had a Jewish mother and you're fighting here together with that man. How can you stand it? Why does he hate us so much?" asked Gabi. "We're on the same side. He wants the Nazis defeated and so do we."

Dominik shrugged again. "It's true. Even here amongst the partisans there are some who hate the Jews. I'm sorry you had to run into Erik. Just keep your distance from him. There are others here who are more welcoming."

Max shuddered again, glancing over his shoulder at the soldier with the angry eyes. One minute Max felt proud to be here, excited at the prospect of helping Dominik and the other partisans. The next minute all his confidence was shattered, as he faced the reality of being hated because he was Jewish. He would not need to be warned about Erik again. He would stay as far away from that man as he possibly could.

Dominik tore a piece of bread from the loaf that Eva had brought and pointed at Max. "You're the one with the gun, right? Can I see it?"

Max nodded and pulled the revolver from the inside pocket of his jacket, holding it up proudly for Dominik to see. Dominik whistled and nodded. "It's a fine gun, a real treasure."

"It doesn't work," said Max. "But you couldn't tell, could you?"

Dominik shook his head. "Pass it here. Let me have a look at it." Dominik took the gun and examined it carefully, holding it up to his eye and turning it over and over in his hands. "It's old. I wonder how it got here."

"I found it buried in the forest," said Max. "Maybe it's from before this war."

Dominik nodded. "Perhaps. But you're right. The firing pin is broken and that's why it doesn't work. I'll tell you what, Max. I'm pretty good with guns. Why don't you leave this one with me? Maybe I can fix it. A gun is the most important possession a partisan soldier can have. If your gun is working, you'll be a real soldier. What do you say?"

The episode with Erik was instantly forgotten. Max's dark eyes shone again with excitement. "Oh yes, please!" he shouted.

Gabi groaned slightly. The thought of Max with a working gun sickened her. It was dangerous enough for him to have the broken one. But guns were now a reality of their lives, whether they liked it or not.

Gabi joined Eva who was walking around the campsite, handing out cups of tea and pieces of bread and cheese. By the time the three children were ready to leave, they had introduced themselves to many of the partisan soldiers and had learned the names of several in return. As they were getting ready to leave, Dominik and Vladimir came to say good-by. "So, my soldiers," said Vladimir. "This was a good visit for you, yes?" Gabi, Max, and Eva nodded enthusiastically. "And it was good for us partisans as well. Perhaps you'll come back."

"Oh yes, we want to," said Gabi, looking over at Dominik.

"Bring us some more supplies and perhaps, on a future visit, I'll have something ready for you as well." Dominik winked at Max.

Chapter Eighteen

June 1944

THE PRISONERS

BY THE TIME SPRING arrived in the village of Olsavica, Gabi, Max, and Eva had returned to the partisans several more times. By now, they knew the route to the partisans on their own. On the nights they visited the campsite, they would often go by way of the Nazis' road. They knew that checking up on the road was part of their job as scouts for the partisans.

Lately, the partisans had done little to interrupt the progress of the road. They were busy with other things. For weeks, they had been sending messages to the Russian army to the east, giving the Russians information on the number of partisan units in the area, their placement, and their willingness to assist in a large uprising. Their goal was to cooperate with the Russian Red Army to free the country from Nazi control. Meanwhile, the partisans were stockpiling food, medicine, arms, and ammunition, gathering intelligence information, and waiting for the right moment to launch a full-scale attack on the Nazis. Vladimir and his troop were planning a major attack on the road, one that they hoped would stop its progress for once and for all.

The route had become very familiar to Gabi, Max, and Eva. The children moved swiftly through the forest toward the road, keeping their heads low and listening for sounds of danger. They would set out on the main path into the woods. About a hundred meters into the forest, they left the path and traveled east, up into the hills behind the farmhouse toward the mountains. Ten minutes later, they would arrive at their destination, crawling on their stomachs for the last twenty meters to avoid being seen. The ridge above the road offered protection from the Nazi soldiers who were patrolling the area. And there the children would sit on the ground, silently watching and listening.

It was there, one day, that Gabi, Max and Eva saw something different. As usual, the Nazi guards were out in full force, watching the perimeter of the road and shouting at the laborers to keep working. But some of the laborers looked quite different on this particular day. In addition to the usual group of farmers and local villagers, Gabi saw that there were other workers on the road. These men were dressed in old battered uniform jackets, much like those worn by the partisans whom the children had befriended. Gabi counted quickly. There were twenty or thirty of these uniformed men working side by side with the local farmers. The Nazi soldiers were guarding these new men much more closely and aggressively. Their guns were held in position, pointed at the workers. The guard dogs stood close by, straining on their leashes and snarling at the uniformed men.

These laborers were obviously prisoners.

Max nudged Gabi's arm and pointed at the workers. He noticed the difference as well. So did Eva, who leaned forward to whisper in Gabi's ear, "They look like partisans."

Gabi nodded. "I don't recognize them," she mouthed back. Gabi's first thought had been that these partisans had been captured from Vladimir's unit. There was some relief in seeing that they were strangers. They must have been captured from some other partisan brigade.

The three children leaned forward, straining to overhear the conversation of the guards. At that moment, one of the Nazi soldiers stepped up to a uniformed worker, blocking his path as he plowed the ground with a spade.

"You're working too slow," the guard shouted. "Speed it up."

The man in question was quite young, no more than twenty years old. His uniform jacket and pants hung in tatters on his stooped body. His face and hands were caked with mud and grime that had spread over his boots and pants. Even from the distance, Gabi could see the gritty sweat that poured down his face.

The Nazi soldier moved closer. "Did you hear what I said? Work faster!"

The young man raised his eyes, stared at the Nazi soldier for a moment, then lowered his head and resumed working at the same pace. He pounded the ground with his spade, up and down in a steady rhythm. Like the sound of a drumbeat, his pounding echoed up to the ridge where the children watched. Gabi felt her own heart beating along with him.

"You think we don't know what you and the others have been up to?" The Nazi guard nudged the soldier with his rifle, bending forward to shout directly into his face. "We know you've been setting fire to our factories and snatching arms from our camps."

Gabi, Max, and Eva watched in wide-eyed horror at the scene unfolding in front of them. Other workers stopped what they were doing and stared in the direction of the Nazi guard. The captured partisan soldier continued digging, bending now and then to move a log out of the way. The expression on his face was grim as the Nazi guard continued his tirade.

"Well, you and your partisan thugs haven't stopped us, have you? Now you're working for Hitler and I'm telling you to work faster!"

In the next moment, the young partisan turned and lunged at the Nazi guard, grabbing him around the throat and twisting his neck with all his might. A powerful roar exploded from the prisoner's lips, echoing through the forest like a trumpet blast. For a moment, no one else moved and then the other Nazis jumped into action. Several ran to pull the prisoner off the Nazi guard, while the other guards surrounded the remaining partisan captives, containing them before they could come to their comrade's aid. The young partisan soldier seemed to have superhuman strength as he fought with his captors. For a moment, Gabi, Max, and Eva thought he might actually wrestle them all to the ground. And then suddenly, a single gunshot rang out in the forest. The young partisan soldier slumped to the ground at the feet of the Nazi guard.

Max gasped and Gabi quickly moved to clasp her hand over his mouth. The Nazi guards stared down at the dead prisoner and then looked over at the other prisoners, each one facing the grisly scene with fury in their eyes.

"Who wants to be next?" shouted a Nazi guard. No one moved. "Get his body out of here and get back to work!"

The children had seen enough. It was time to get to the partisan campsite and report on what they had just witnessed.

Chapter Nineteen

PLANNING FOR BATTLE

SILENTLY, the children left the ridge above the road and began to run quickly in the direction of the partisan camp. They knew that what they had observed on the road was of vital importance to their friends. Out of breath, they arrived at the campsite and were greeted by Dominik.

"Whoa, slow down," said Dominik. "Catch your breath. Why the speed?" Dominik was seated by a fire pit, polishing his rifle. He had taken it apart and was cleaning each piece before carefully reassembling the weapon. Max eyed Dominik enviously. Max had asked Dominik several times about the progress of the repairs on his own gun. Each time, Dominik told Max to be patient. It would take time to make the gun work right.

Gabi's heart was still pounding and her lungs were aching from the run through the forest. It took a minute to catch her breath before she could answer Dominik. "Get Vladimir," she said. "We've seen something on the road that he needs to know about."

Dominik looked at the serious faces of the children. Without another word, he rose and moved to the other side of the campsite where Vladimir was deep in conversation with a number of soldiers. Dominik interrupted the discussion, and the two of them moved quickly over to where the children stood.

"Dominik says you have news," said Vladimir.

Gabi, Max, and Eva told Vladimir about the prisoners they had seen working on the road. They described this new group of laborers, how they were dressed and how much more harshly they were treated by the Nazis. Finally, they described the young soldier who had lunged at the Nazi guard, only to be shot dead.

When the children finished speaking, Vladimir looked grim. "How many prisoners did you say there were?" he asked.

"At least twenty, maybe thirty," replied Eva.

Vladimir nodded. "There was a report over the radio, earlier yesterday, of a battalion of partisans that was attacked in the woods near the town of Brezno, west of here. Dozens were killed in the raid, but some were taken captive. These must be the prisoners you saw. It sounds like our comrades are now in the hands of the Nazis."

"What do you think will happen to them?" asked Max.

Vladimir paused. "They'll be used to work on the road. And when they are no longer useful to the Nazis, they will be killed."

There was silence in the campsite. Then Vladimir continued talking. "We must do something," he said, raising his voice. "We will not stand by and let our comrades be killed." He nodded to the soldiers who were standing around him.

"We will make this part of our larger plan." Then Vladimir turned and walked away.

The other soldiers quickly dispersed. Gabi, Max, and Eva were left standing with Dominik. Max was the first to break the silence. "What does Vladimir mean when he says we must do something?" he asked. "And what kind of larger plan is he talking about?"

Dominik paused. "There have been plans for some time," he said slowly. "We've learned through our radio reports that the Russians have promised to send troops, thousands of Red Army soldiers, to help us free our country from Nazi rule. We've been waiting for these Russian reinforcements, so we too can launch our attack on the Nazis. But Vladimir won't wait to attack the road, if he thinks partisan soldiers are in danger of being killed."

Gabi's head was reeling. Vladimir and his army were going to attempt to free the partisan prisoners. It was all part of some larger plan to revolt against the Nazis. And they had stumbled into the middle of it and provided a key piece of information about the partisan prisoners.

"When will all this happen?" asked Max.

"I'm not sure," Dominik replied. "That's for Vladimir to decide. It will be soon. And now that we know about the prisoners, it could be even sooner. But I do know this," he continued, staring solemnly at the three children. "It will be dangerous. The three of you should probably stay away from here for a while."

Ignoring Dominik's warning, Max's eyes shone with excitement. "We're coming back," Max said. "I want to be here when there's a battle. Tell us we can come, Dominik."

Dominik paused. "The information you brought us today is important. Vladimir knows that. We'll have to see about future visits. For now, you'd better get out of here. I think you've spied enough for one day."

Gabi, Eva, and Max said good-by to Dominik and left the campsite. They spoke little as they walked back through the forest to the farmhouse, lost in their own thoughts. Eva wondered what medicine and food she might be able to slip past her grandmother to bring to the partisans on their next visit. If there was going to be a battle, they would need those supplies. Max hoped he would be able to go along on the raid and wondered if his gun would be ready. He wanted to fight, side by side with Dominik. As for Gabi, her heart was filled with both exhilaration and dread. There was such danger here in the forest. This was the first time in her life she had seen someone killed in front of her eyes and it terrified her. Now, with this pending battle, there was to be even more danger. Would she be brave enough to join in? On the other hand, she felt the thrill of being alive and part of the action. This was a thousand times better than waiting in the hay barn for the war to end.

Mama must not know about these recent developments. If she knew that the partisans were about to stage an attack, it would certainly be the end of their visits to the forest. No, this was something Gabi, Max, and Eva would keep to themselves.

Chapter Twenty

NAZIS IN THE VILLAGE

THE SNOW HAD LONG since melted in the mountains. Long, rapidly flowing streams wound their way down the hillsides and through the villages below, leaving muddy paths and trails behind. Gabi, Max, and Eva tried to get back to the forest one night, but their feet sank in the mud as if it were quick sand. In the end, they had to turn back.

"Besides," said Mama. "You'll leave footprints that might lead people back here to the farmhouse. It's too dangerous." Mama looked relieved. She welcomed any opportunity to keep the children inside. But for Gabi and Max, it felt like a prison sentence. For the time being, the children had to remain patient. They could only daydream about what was happening with the partisans in the woods.

One day, several weeks later, Gabi and Max sat in the hayloft, playing a word game to pass the time. "Okay, Max. I'm thinking of something that is green," said Gabi impatiently, as she yawned and looked around. The game seemed so trivial in light of what she knew was being planned in the forest. But there was no other way to pass the time in the hayloft.

"It has to be in the barn, Gabi," complained Max. "Remember, I have to be able to see it."

"I know the rules," said Gabi, wearily. "I know how to —"

At the sound of loud voices, the children suddenly froze. They were deep men's voices, moving closer and closer, barking orders and commands in German.

"What is that?" cried Max, scrambling over to the outside wall of the barn. He pushed his glasses up on his nose and pressed his face against a crack in the barn board, straining to identify the sounds.

"Max, come away from the wall," whispered Mama, desperately pulling on her nephew's sleeve.

"Wait," whispered Max, "I want to see what's going on." The sounds grew louder, until it seemed as though the voices were right beside the barn, directly below their hiding place. Gabi crawled over next to Max, so she, too, could peer out through a slit in the wall. Mama gasped and shook her head furiously, her eyes pleading with her children to come closer to her. Gabi ignored her mother, as she squinted through the boards at the road below.

Dozens of Nazi soldiers were marching in both directions, some toward the village and others away from it. They saluted one another with an outstretched arm, the symbol of greeting used by all of Hitler's followers. As they marched, their arms swung stiffly back and forth and their legs lifted in rigid unison. Gabi had seen this march before and it terrified her.

Max grabbed Gabi's arm and pointed below. Two

soldiers stood on the road close to the barn, directly below the hayloft, inspecting the army as it passed. They seemed to be in charge of the march, nodding briefly to the soldiers. As the groups of soldiers disappeared in all directions, the two commanding officers spoke to each other in rapid German. Their words were clipped and sharp. Because they spoke so quickly, Gabi had difficulty following their conversation. Gabi could not understand why the Nazi soldiers were here in the village. She turned to Mama, whose face had gone quite pale.

"Mama," she mouthed, gesturing toward the soldiers below. "What are they saying?"

Mama shook her head and motioned frantically with her hands for Gabi and Max to be still. Desperately, she signaled to the children to move away from the barn wall. But Gabi and Max were glued to their spots by the wall and continued to watch through the cracks.

Finally, the two soldiers saluted and began to walk in opposite directions. One officer glanced up toward the barn before he moved away. Gabi caught her breath, as his eyes seemed to line up directly with her own. She fell away from the wall, shaking uncontrollably. Did she only imagine it or had she actually looked into the eyes of the Nazi soldier? And had he looked straight back at her?

No one moved in the barn. Nobody breathed and not a word was whispered. Minutes passed — minutes that felt like hours — as the sound of the soldiers' marching feet gradually grew softer, until they disappeared.

"That was so close," said Max, finally. "I don't think he

saw us, Gabi."

Gabi was still shaking as she sat forward to face her mother. "Mama, what were the soldiers saying? I couldn't understand everything."

Mama still looked pale and dazed. "They said … they said the road is going well. The extra troops will soon be here. They said Hitler's armies will move in against the Russians and wipe them out." Her voice faded into a whisper. "They said it would be a glorious victory."

Mr. Kos appeared later that evening to let them out into the family home. Sitting around the kitchen table, Mama talked with Mr. Kos about what she had heard. Mrs. Kos no longer joined them in the kitchen these days. She fed everyone quickly. And then, just as quickly, she retired to her bedroom. Everyone seemed to agree that the less contact she had with Gabi, Max, and Mama, the better it was for all of them. Joseph arrived that night, bringing some extra clothing and food.

"The soldiers made it sound as if Hitler is winning the war. I cannot imagine what will happen if the Nazis win," said Mama, shaking her head sorrowfully.

"It's not true, Judith," insisted Joseph. "Don't believe what the Nazis are saying. We hear other reports, late at night on the radio — reports from other countries. Just last month, the Americans along with the British and Canadians landed in Normandy, France and launched a huge attack. They have entered Paris and are moving to reclaim other parts of Europe. The Allies are powerful — more powerful than the Nazis. It's only a matter of time before Hitler must surrender. The road they are building outside this village is their last attempt to bring the armies up to this part of the country. But they will fail, I am certain. Even the partisans are banding together to create more damage to the Nazis. The war will end soon and Hitler will be destroyed."

Gabi looked from her mother to Joseph and back again. What could she believe? She too had heard the soldiers underneath the barn. They spoke with such determination and certainty. On the other hand, she knew what the partisans were planning. They were intent on slowing down the progress of the Nazis until the Russians and the Americans arrived. She desperately wanted to believe the partisans would be successful.

"But your experience today is a warning that we must double our efforts to keep you safe," continued Mr. Kos. "During the day, you must only talk in whispers, no more speaking aloud." Then he looked directly at Gabi, Max, and Eva. "And I'm afraid there will be no more night walks either. It's simply too dangerous now for you to leave the barn."

"But," began Gabi. "This information is so important. The partisans need to know that the Nazi soldiers were in the village today."

The look on Mama's face stopped her from saying any more. Gabi looked over at Max and Eva and nodded solemnly.

Chapter Twenty-one

August 1944

RETURN TO THE PARTISANS

GABI AND MAX knew they had to get back to the forest as soon as they could. But now it was more difficult than ever to convince Mama to let them go.

It was Max who finally wore Mama down. He pleaded and begged to go back to the forest. Finally, he threatened to stop eating if Mama did not let them out. That was the last straw. They were already close to wasting away, because nutritious food had become so scarce. Mama could count the ribs sticking out on Max's chest when he pulled off his shirt to wash. Because she could not stand the thought of Max starving himself on purpose, she finally relented.

When Gabi, Max, and Eva reached the partisan camp-site this time, it seemed as if everything had changed. The casual attitude of the soldiers had been replaced with an urgent and serious determination. There was excitement and tension in the air.

"Things are happening here tonight. The three of you will have to stay out of our way," said Dominik when he saw

Gabi, Max, and Eva.

"We have some more news for you," said Gabi, determined to get his attention. "There were many Nazi soldiers in the village last week and we overheard their conversations."

Dominik listened closely as Gabi described the exchange between the Nazi soldiers below the barn almost a week earlier. He immediately summoned Vladimir and Gabi repeated the conversation.

Vladimir shook his head. "We know the Nazis are increasing their efforts to destroy us. We also know about the Allies landing in France. It's being called D-Day, the battle of Normandy. It's a huge blow to the Nazi forces."

Dominik interrupted. "And we know that just last month a group of Germans tried to assassinate Hitler. They failed, but do you realize what this means? The Nazis are losing support from their own people."

Vladimir nodded. "We can't wait any longer for the Russians to send their troops," he added grimly. "Our own partisan soldiers are being held prisoner and we must help them."

Gabi looked around. There was more activity in the partisan campsite than she had ever seen before. The partisans seemed to be getting ready for battle, checking weapons and gathering equipment. Suddenly, a group of soldiers began to cheer and chant. Waving their rifles in the air, they yelled for the total destruction of the Nazi armies. Max joined in, shouting at the top of his lungs.

Vladimir looked down at the children and smiled wryly. "So, my young soldiers, you came back to us just at the right time. Are you ready to fight?"

Gabi, Max, and Eva looked at each other with growing expectation.

"Tonight, we are going out to the road. We will free our comrades who are being held captive. And we will bomb the road and put an end to more Nazi troops in this area. Will you join us in battle, my young soldiers?"

This was the opportunity for which the children had been waiting. Up until now, they had done small things to help the partisans, bringing them food and the occasional information. But now they had the opportunity to participate in some real action.

"Will you really let us come with you?" asked Max breathlessly.

Vladimir nodded. "The first time I brought Dominik along on a raid, he wasn't much older than you. The three of you are brave enough to be partisans. Of course, you can join us. But listen to me carefully. You will carry some equipment for us and stay at the rear, away from the battle." Vladimir continued giving instructions. "You'll do exactly what you are told to do and when you are told to do it. There is no room for mistakes. I give the commands and you, my soldiers, must follow them. Is that clear?"

And then Vladimir disappeared, moving swiftly through the campsite, giving orders to his soldiers. Dominik moved the children off to one side, telling them to wait for him to return with their orders. Left alone, Gabi, Max, and Eva stared at each other for several seconds.

"Well," said Max, "this is what we've been waiting for."

He spoke uneasily.

"Are you scared?" asked Eva.

Gabi nodded. "Terrified."

"Me too," Eva said.

"We can't think about being scared right now," Gabi continued. "We must think about why we're here. I'm here for Papa and for my cousin Magda and for all my friends and family who have been taken away."

"I'm doing this for my parents," said Max.

Eva looked straight at Gabi without blinking. "And I'm doing it for both of you."

Max, Gabi, and Eva joined hands for a moment and stood together, three young friends bonded together by unusual events.

And then, Dominik appeared again to take charge. "Gabi," he said. "You can help carry the radio on your back. We need to be in contact with the other partisan troops as we advance. Eva, you and Max will carry these backpacks filled with extra ammunition. The soldiers will come to you, when they need to reload their weapons. Oh, and one more thing," he said, reaching into his own back pocket, "I think this belongs to you, Max." Dominik withdrew a gun and placed it in Max's hands. "I told you I was pretty good at fixing these things. It's working now, Max. And it's all yours. So be careful."

"I really am a soldier now, Gabi," said Max as he held the gun to his eye, pretending to take aim.

"There are no bullets in it right now," added Dominik. "But you keep it safe, Max. Remember, a gun is the most important thing a soldier can have. You may need it some time."

Gabi gulped hard as she tried to smile at Max. She wasn't sure what made her more anxious, the thought of Max with a gun or the fact that she was going on a partisan raid. But there was no time left to think about any of that. Vladimir was ordering the children to move forward and they had to fall quickly in line behind the soldiers. The partisan troops moved out of the campsite and into the dark forest.

Chapter Twenty-two

AN EXPLOSION IN THE FOREST

MOVING SWIFTLY, the partisan troop made its way through the woods, heading toward the Nazi road. The radio tied to Gabi's back was heavy. It smacked against trees and bushes, as Gabi struggled to keep up with the soldiers. Dominik kept track of the three young people, appearing every few minutes to urge them forward.

"Are you alright?" Dominik whispered, catching Gabi by the arm as she stumbled over a hidden rut in the forest floor. Maybe it had been a mistake to have Gabi carry the radio. Dominik hadn't realized how weakened she was. But there was no time to change the plan.

"I'm … fine." Talking was an effort and Gabi needed to focus on walking. She bent her head, gulped in air, and tried to think only about putting one foot in front of the other as quickly as she could.

Carrying the backpacks, Max and Eva seemed to be having an easier time. Eva was having no difficulty keeping up. She was a strong farm girl, used to the rough wooded terrain. And Max had been waiting for this moment. He wanted to attack the Nazis — the soldiers who had taken his parents away from him, the soldiers whom he and Gabi had met on the road the day they arrived in the village. In his mind, they blended together as the enemy. With bullets in his backpack and a gun in his pocket, he was determined to fight.

Suddenly, there was a signal from up ahead. One by one, like dominoes, the soldiers dropped to the ground. Gabi, Max, and Eva followed. For the rest of the way, they all crawled on the ground, heads down, stomachs hugging the earth. Like ants edging toward the top of an anthill, the partisan army inched forward until they could see over the top of the ridge. The Nazi road lay before them, about fifty meters away.

Below, the partisan prisoners were hard at work on the road, laboring side by side with the villagers. Totally unaware of the oncoming attack, there were approximately fifty Nazi soldiers on guard.

Dominik motioned the children to move closer to him. With their heads pressed together, he whispered to them. "The three of you will stay here. Don't even think about moving," he added, noting the tinge of disappointment in Max's eyes. "Is that clear?"

Gabi nodded with relief. As much as she wanted to be with these courageous fighters, she didn't want to get too close to the shooting.

Dominik continued whispering instructions. "Gabi, give me the radio. I need to let the other partisan units in the area know that we are ready to strike."

Gabi removed the radio from her back and passed it

carefully to Dominik. Dominik clicked it on and waited to make contact with another partisan troop. Speaking softly and urgently, he whispered their location into the receiver. Then he signed off, passed the radio back to Gabi, and signaled to Vladimir across the hill.

Vladimir had been waiting for this sign from Dominik. Seconds later, the first shots were fired in the forest. And then, chaos broke out. A group of partisan fighters ran from the protection of the ridge down toward the road. Others provided the cover, firing at the enemy and discharging grenades onto the road. As planned, the attack was a complete surprise, begun at a perfect moment when the Nazis had moved the partisan prisoners and the other workers on the road to one side, so that bulldozers could move in to do some clearing. Vladimir did not want to endanger the lives of the workers.

Grenades exploded, lighting up the sky. Gunshots blasted and whizzed in all directions. Artillery fire thundered through the forest. Smoke filled the air, choking Gabi's lungs. She reached out for Max and Eva, encircling both of them with one arm. They all coughed and gasped, struggling to breathe as the battle unfolded.

The instant the partisan attack began, the prisoners on the road scattered, sprinting for protection in the forest. Too busy protecting themselves, the Nazis did not stop them. At first, it seemed there was little the Nazis could do to halt the partisan advance. Nazi soldiers ran from the battleground toward the forest, grabbing their guns and shooting into the air. Unable to see their attackers, they were disoriented and disorganized, no match for the well-prepared partisans.

Vladimir led the partisan attack. He pressed forward, dodging behind tree stumps, jumping out to fire at the Nazis on the road, and then moving forward again. Gabi gasped as Vladimir stumbled once, then quickly regained his footing, and plowed forward again. He signaled to his troops to follow and swiftly they advanced with him. Gabi watched Nazi after Nazi fall, hit by partisan fire.

Still the Nazis would not give up. Slowly, they began to regroup and returned the fire more defiantly. Gabi raised her head slightly and watched as a group of Nazis turned a searchlight in the direction of the forest, lighting up the woods and trying to expose the partisans. Vladimir quickly took aim with his machine gun, shattering the light and sending the Nazis scattering once more.

Suddenly, Gabi felt Max stiffen beside her. He grabbed Gabi's arm and shouted above the burst of gunfire, "Look at Dominik. I think he's in trouble."

Sure enough, Dominik seemed to be struggling. It wasn't that he was hurt. It looked as if his gun were jammed. He repeatedly pounded the barrel of his gun with his fists and thumped the butt of the rifle against the ground.

Up ahead, a small group of armed Nazi soldiers began to advance toward the forest. They moved in a tight pack, unleashing a furious barrage of gunfire toward the partisans. Gabi ducked her head again as bullets whizzed by, then looked up anxiously to see the Nazis pressing forward toward the spot where Dominik lay. Meanwhile, Dominik continued to bang his rifle against the ground to no avail. In another few minutes, the Nazis would be upon him.

"I've got to help Dominik," shouted Max as he reached into his pocket to withdraw his gun. Max twisted his backpack off his shoulders and loaded his gun with ammunition. Clutching his revolver, he began to move in Dominik's direction. Gabi yanked him hard by the arm.

"No!" she shouted. "You heard what Dominik said. We have to stay here. Those are our orders."

Max pulled his arm free. "Stay here with Eva. I'll be careful. I promise."

Before Gabi could say another word, Max had slithered off toward Dominik. Keeping his head as close to the ground as he could, he inched his way across the ridge. I have to get to Dominik, thought Max. The Nazis are going to hurt him. He's in trouble and I have a gun. In that moment, nothing else mattered to Max. He forgot both the danger and the orders. Holding his gun ahead of him in one hand, he crawled forward toward Dominik. Twenty more meters and I'll reach him, Max thought. Ten more meters, then five, and suddenly he was next to Dominik.

"Max, I ordered you to stay put," shouted Dominik. He grabbed Max roughly and pulled him over, shielding his head from the flying bullets. "What do you think you are doing?"

The small group of Nazis was advancing steadily. Max said nothing. Here was his moment. He would raise the gun and shoot at the enemy. He would become a real soldier. He swallowed hard as the blood pounded in his head and his breathing became rapid. He couldn't move. Why don't I shoot, he thought. This is what I've been waiting for. Each shot I fire will be a shot for my mother, father, and sister — a shot that might set them free — a shot that might bring them back to me. Still Max did nothing.

"Max," shouted Dominik. "Give me your gun."

Max looked up at Dominik's face, took a deep breath, and turned the revolver over to Dominik. Dominik hesitated for only a second. Then he grabbed the gun, pushed Max's head down, and began firing at the approaching Nazis.

In the final moments of the attack on the road, Vladimir gave the command to destroy all remaining Nazi equipment. Grenades were lobbed into the air, finding their mark on the bulldozers that were clearing the forest to make way for the road. Seconds later, a great explosion thundered through the forest, lighting up the night sky like a brilliant fireworks display. And then there was silence.

When Gabi lifted her head again, she could view the scene on the road. Through the smoky fog and debris, it looked as though the road had been hit hard. The bombs and grenades had found their mark. The Nazis' machinery had been destroyed. Gravel, rocks, twisted tree stumps, and debris were scattered everywhere on the disheveled road site.

Cheers rumbled across the forest ridge as the partisans lifted their guns and shouted their victory roar. Their cheers were joined by the voices of the partisan prisoners who had been freed in the battle. Then, from the distance came the sound of approaching machine guns. Nazi reinforcements were closing in. A moment later, Vladimir sounded the signal to retreat.

Chapter Twenty-three

BACK TO THE CAMPSITE

DOMINIK MOTIONED TO GABI, Max, and Eva to withdraw. Leading the way, he moved in the direction of the partisan campsite with the three young people close behind.

Gabi still felt fear pulsing through her body. The distant machine gunfire was enough to warn her that, while this raid might have been a success, danger was not far behind. The Nazis would now be out for revenge. The woods were pitch black and, with everyone on the run, it was easy to lose your way. Gabi stumbled and tripped over a fallen log, plunging head forward onto the ground, and landing with a loud thud. The radio backpack flew over Gabi's head and bounced against a large tree a few meters away.

Out of nowhere, Dominik appeared one more time. "I'll help you," he whispered, bending to retrieve the radio and shifting it onto his own back. "I know where we are," he said, pulling Gabi to her feet. "I've been through this part of the forest lots of times. Just stay right behind me, in my path." Gabi nodded and fell into step behind Dominik. He zigzagged this way and that, avoiding the swampy mud puddles, jagged tree stumps, and even the rocks, half hidden by dirt and leaves.

They finally approached the partisan camp and collapsed to the ground, breathing heavily. Gabi's chest ached, but that was not her greatest pain. She sat up and glanced down at her knee, cut and bleeding. She must have injured herself when she fell during the retreat from the raid. At the time, Gabi had been so intent on following Dominik back to the campsite, she hadn't even noticed the pain. But now, her knee burned and throbbed.

"Ouch! That looks terrible. Are you okay?" Eva propped herself on one elbow and looked over at Gabi's knee.

Gabi swallowed hard and nodded. She didn't want to complain, not after the courage everyone else had displayed. This injury seemed so trivial. Still, her knee hurt so much that she flinched from the pain. Dominik was watching from across the campsite and quickly moved close to kneel beside Gabi.

"That's quite an injury," he said, "but nothing we can't fix here." Dominik withdrew a small penknife from his back pocket and quickly cut the material of Gabi's overalls away from her knee. Then he opened his canteen and poured some clean water over the wound.

Gabi winced and tried to blink back the tears. "Are you the medic too?" she asked as Dominik wrapped a clean handkerchief around Gabi's knee and tied it expertly. He smiled at her and nodded. "I'm whatever I need to be. You'll have to be careful with that," he added pointing at Gabi's knee. "Make sure you keep it clean. These wounds can easily become infected and then you'll be in real trouble." Gabi nodded and gently moved her leg up and down.

"What's the matter with you?" asked Dominik, looking over at Max. Max had been silent and dejected ever since the soldiers had withdrawn from the Nazi road. "Have you been injured too?"

Max shook his head and looked down. Suddenly, he sat forward. "I let everyone down," he blurted. "I didn't use my gun at all. I was supposed to shoot and I didn't do anything. I'm not really a soldier." Max remembered how, in those final moments on the ridge overlooking the advancing Nazi group, he had frozen.

Dominik sat back on his heels and looked over at Max. "What are you talking about?" he asked sharply. Dominik understood this spirited young boy. "When I first came here, all I wanted to do was kill the Nazis who killed my parents. Don't get me wrong," Dominik added quickly. "I still do. But I'm part of an army now, a member of a troop. And what my troop needs is even more important than what I want to do. You saved my life tonight, Max. Those Nazis would have been on me in minutes. If you hadn't crawled over and given me your gun, who knows what might have happened. I owe you my life." Dominik reached into his own pocket and withdrew Max's gun. "Here," said Dominik. "This still belongs to you."

Max hesitated a moment before reaching for the revolver. "But I wanted to shoot the Nazis myself," he continued.

"We all want to get back at the enemy," said Dominik.

"And maybe that time will come for you, Max. But in the meantime, you need to know that you were a good soldier tonight. You did what was needed. Vladimir said he would have you along on a mission anytime."

Max's face brightened and he looked up at Dominik. "He said that?"

Dominik nodded and looked over at Gabi and Eva. "You have all shared in our raid. You can now consider yourselves partisans."

Chapter Twenty-four

October 1944

AMBUSH

IN THE MONTHS THAT FOLLOWED, it became impossible for Gabi, Eva, and Max to continue their night scouting for the partisans. Heavy Nazi patrols were now a regular occurrence in the village, making it too dangerous for Gabi and Max to leave their hiding place.

Gabi and her family listened to the radio broadcasts each night, as they sat in the kitchen with Mr. Kos. While the local partisans had managed to free their fellow soldiers held captive on the road site, the toll on the general partisan population had been enormous. Thousands of partisan fighters in regiments across the country had been killed during the widespread attacks on the Nazis. Despite American efforts to assist the partisan uprising by airlifting weapons and ammunition, the Nazis managed to occupy the eastern part of Czechoslovakia by September 1944. Nazi retaliation was swift. Thousands of Slovak citizens were killed. More Jews were being deported to concentration camps. The Russian army, waiting in the mountains, witnessed the tragedy and did nothing at the time. Their promised troops never arrived.

"Partisan units are still battling across the country, trying to hold out against the Nazis until the Russians arrive," said Mr. Kos one night. These days, only a small candle burned on the kitchen table when the family gathered at night. Mrs. Kos had added extra material to the window curtains to keep the light from being visible from the outside. No one wanted to draw attention to the farmhouse.

Mama nodded. "Yes, we can hear bombing in the forest almost daily."

"I'll bet the partisans are setting more land mines," said Max with a smile. He missed scouting for the soldiers.

Gabi pushed her hair back off her forehead and wiped the sweat from her brow. Here in this sealed up kitchen, it was difficult to imagine the cool fall air outside. It would soon be winter and the snow would keep them from entering the woods again. Yes, she thought, it was time to get back to the forest and visit the partisans.

The opportunity did not arise until many weeks later. And it was Joseph who suggested it when he arrived one night with an armload of extra clothing.

"I've gathered these clothes for your partisan friends," said Joseph. "We're praying that the war won't go into another winter. But if it does, your friends will need these things."

Gabi looked over at Mama, who hesitated and then nodded her head.

"Perhaps the Kos family will be able to spare some extra food to go with that clothing," she said. By now, even Mama recognized how important the partisans were. If her family were to survive in these final days, they would need the help of the partisans battling on their behalf.

And so, several days later, when the road was clear, Gabi, Max, and Eva made their way back to the forest to see the partisans. This time, it was difficult to locate them in the thick forest. By now, the partisan soldiers had changed campsites several times to avoid Nazi detection. Gabi, Max, and Eva were close to giving up, when a patrolling group of partisans discovered them and lead them to the new camp. There, the children were warmly greeted. The partisans appreciated the clothes and extra food. Gabi, Max, and Eva were able to spend some time with Dominik by the fire.

"Joseph heard about a revolt in the Auschwitz concentration camp," said Gabi. "A group of Jewish prisoners destroyed a part of the camp. All the reports say that Germany is losing the war."

"Yes," agreed Dominik. "We know about a revolt in Auschwitz. We also know that the Russian armies liberated a concentration camp called Majdanek. The reports were terrible. Thousands of Jews had been killed there and the ones who were left were barely strong enough to stand or walk."

Gabi struggled with what she was hearing. It was painful to imagine thousands of people being put to death in one place. And if this was happening in one concentration camp, then what was happening in all the others? Instinctively, Gabi reached out to touch Max's hand. He glanced at her and swallowed hard. These days, Max rarely spoke about his own family, but Gabi knew that they were never far from his thoughts.

"But we're making headway," Dominik continued. "Vladimir says that we will continue to fight the Nazi forces and before long we will defeat them all. There are partisan units all over Europe that are battling the Nazis and winning. One group in Poland blew up a German military train. Each victory moves us closer to the end of the war. Before we know it …" Dominik paused mid-sentence and sat up suddenly, listening intently for a moment to a sound coming from the woods. "Did you hear that?" he asked.

"I think it's just the wind," said Max. A cool fall air was blowing throughout the forest, a sign that colder weather was approaching.

Dominik shrugged. "Maybe I'm just jittery," he said and turned back to the children. Then he sat up again. "No, listen. There it is again." Gabi listened. There were always noises in the forest. Dominik looked worried. "Wait here," he continued. "I think I'll go check on the soldiers who are on sentry duty. We can never be too careful these days."

One moment the children were sitting, listening to Dominik talk about partisan victories and the next moment a young partisan soldier came flying into the camp. Suddenly there was chaos everywhere.

"Everyone scatter! Nazi troops are approaching!" The soldier yelled as he ran through the camp. Vladimir was not far behind, shouting commands as he ran through the campsite. Dominik disappeared, as all the partisan soldiers flew into action. Several grabbed communication equipment and took off into the forest. Others made for the ammunition, snatching guns and grenades before scattering into the woods. Gabi, Max, and Eva stared for a split second, paralyzed with fear, not knowing what they should do.

And then Dominik reappeared. "Run, now!" he ordered. "Run for your lives, soldiers!" And so Gabi, Max, and Eva ran. They ran with all their might and they did not look back. They ran through the forest, past bushes and over fallen logs. The tree branches whipped past Gabi's face, blinding her at times as she scrambled to keep up with her cousin and Eva. The three of them knew they could not be separated. Sweat poured from Gabi's face. And still she ran, all the while listening for the sounds of the guns and grenades behind her. It was hard to tell if they came from partisan friends or Nazi enemies. But the children could not slow down to check.

Gabi and Max followed behind Eva. Here in the woods, she was their guide. She knew every inch of these mountains and now they would rely on her to lead them to a safe place. At one point, Eva ducked behind a large rock, pushing Gabi and Max down next to her. There they cowered, as the sound of marching boots moved ever closer in the forest. When the coast was clear, they continued to run.

Max suddenly stumbled next to Gabi, dropping to the ground and calling out to her. "Wait! I've lost my glasses. I can't see!"

Gabi stopped, turning frantically to her young cousin. Max was helpless without his glasses. Without them, there was no way he could move through these treacherous woods. Gabi called for Eva to stop and then dropped to the ground next to Max.

"Where are they?" Max cried desperately, as his hands moved over the forest floor. Eva joined Gabi on her knees. All three began to search through the branches, leaves, and dirt for Max's glasses. The children knew how dangerous it was to linger. With each passing moment, the night sky was turning brighter. In the early morning light, there was a greater risk that they might be found. The children continued to search, dropping face forward in the mud whenever they heard a noise.

"I've got them," Eva finally cried out. Triumphantly, she held up Max's glasses and passed them to him. Max grabbed them, gratefully, then stood with Gabi and Eva and began to run again. They had lost precious time and light was starting to dawn.

They ran on and on, ducking behind trees and rocks and then emerging to run some more. And finally, when Gabi felt like she could run no further, Eva began to slow down and creep along the forest floor. Max bent to follow and motioned Gabi to do the same. Eva turned, placing a finger on her lips to silence the other two. The children stopped and listened in the dawning light.

Chapter Twenty-five

THE COW HERD

AT FIRST, everything seemed peaceful. Signs of light began to penetrate between the tree branches overhead. In the woods, the only sounds Gabi could make out were the chirping of birds and the faint trickling of a stream from the woods behind them. And then, she heard it — the light jingle of cowbells, accompanied by the low sound of a cow herder's command.

Eva pointed ahead towards the clearing. Max and Gabi strained to make out shapes through the thick brush. She now realized where Eva had brought them. Somehow, they had doubled back through the woods and were on the hill, directly above the Kos farmhouse. Down below, on the hillside, Mr. Kos was tending his herd of cows, having brought them out to the pasture to graze for the day.

Eva placed her finger across her lips and motioned for Max and Gabi to crouch down and follow her as she crept out of the woods and across the field. Max and Gabi nodded. Together the three moved slowly out of the forest, away from the protective cover of the trees.

Gabi, Eva, and Max were now exposed in the open

field. Creeping on all fours, the children moved forward toward Mr. Kos and the cows, keeping their heads as low as possible. They still listened for sounds of approaching soldiers. So far, the coast was clear. Another few yards and the children reached the herd and waved to Mr. Kos.

"Evichka!" exclaimed Mr. Kos, spotting his grand-daughter first. "Max, Gabi! Why are you here in the field in the daylight? This is terribly dangerous."

"Grandpa," Eva cried. "There was a raid on the partisan camp. The Nazis were everywhere. We've been running and running. I knew you'd be here, so that's why we came. I didn't know what else to do."

Mr. Kos immediately took charge. "Move amongst the herd, as if you are helping me," he ordered. "I'm going to bring the cows back to the barn, along with the three of you. My herd will provide the cover." Without hesitation, Gabi, Max, and Eva walked into the herd of cows. Eva moved closer to where Mr. Kos was standing, as if this would offer extra protection.

It was not hard to walk among the cattle. Gabi had grown up with cows on her own farm. She knew farm animals. She had hand-fed and milked cows from the time she was a young child. She had watched cows being born and helped in the birthing process. Gabi whistled, guiding the herd in the right direction and Max imitated her. Being in the midst of the cow herd felt familiar to Gabi. It was peaceful and protective, as if they were among old friends. Gabi picked up a long stick lying on the ground and began to walk with it. Making low whistling sounds, she moved the cows along skillfully. Mr. Kos nodded with approval.

With the help of the three children, it took no time at all to round up the cows and begin to walk them down the hill toward the village. Closer and closer, they came to the barn and to their hiding place. With Mr. Kos up ahead in the front, Gabi held her breath, counting the steps until they would be at the gate. She glanced reassuringly at Max and he nodded back. Next to her, Eva brushed past her arm and squeezed her hand quickly as she passed. A few more steps and they would be back at the Kos farmhouse.

Intent on getting back into the safety of the barn, Gabi barely saw the Nazi patrol approaching. Mr. Kos was the first to alert them to the Nazi soldiers. "Children," he said urgently. "Move faster." Gabi turned and saw a dozen soldiers moving swiftly across the field.

Armed and on alert, the soldiers pointed their guns ahead and, even from this distance, Gabi could see the grim determination on their faces. They were on the hunt and she felt like their prey. Max continued to whistle, while Eva moved closer to her grandfather. Up ahead, Mr. Kos began to move the cows more quickly, as if he thought he could outrun the soldiers and get Gabi and Max back into the farmhouse.

Gabi glanced behind her. The soldiers were moving rapidly over the pasture and would reach them in seconds. Gabi looked up ahead at the barn, agonizing at how close they were to the safety of the hayloft. She glanced up at their hiding place. Could Mama see the Nazi soldiers coming up behind them? Max stopped his whistling and glanced anxiously at Gabi. Eva turned to her grandfather.

"Let me do the talking," he ordered. "Don't say a word." The children nodded as the soldiers began to shout at them from behind.

Chapter Twenty-six

ENCOUNTER IN THE FIELD

"HALT!" A soldier's voice bellowed from the distance. "Stand still and don't move."

Mr. Kos and the children came to an abrupt stop as the Nazi soldiers surrounded them. The tall Nazi officer towered over them, his eyes threatening. "There are partisan criminals here in the woods. We've just broken up their camp," he announced. "The outlaws got away." The Nazi commander spat the words out as if they were poison on his lips. "But, believe me, they won't get far. We will find those animals and we will kill every one of them. You, farmer, did you see anyone come by here?"

"No, sir," replied Mr. Kos, adjusting his cap with pretended confidence. "I've been here for an hour and I have seen no one. My cows are restless and I'm trying to bring them back to the barn."

The commander ignored Mr. Kos's efforts to reassure him. "My soldiers are moving into this village to put down these partisan revolts once and for all. We'll root out the criminals in this area and get rid of them, you can be sure of that!"

Mr. Kos nodded. "Yes, sir. I understand, sir."

In spite of her fear, Gabi listened intently to what was being said. The Nazi patrol was stationing itself inside the village. That would make their situation even more dangerous. Not only would it be impossible for Gabi and Max to venture outside their hiding place, but they would have to be even more careful inside not to draw attention to the Kos farm. That is, if they ever managed to return to the barn. The soldier leading the Nazi patrol seemed to be finished with Mr. Kos.

"What is your name?" the Nazi officer barked as he turned to Gabi. When Mr. Kos tried to interrupt, the officer pushed him aside. Gabi opened her mouth and closed it again. She looked up at the soldier and caught her breath. It was the same soldier whom she had seen outside, through the cracks of their barn wall months before, the one whose eyes had seemed to look back at her.

"I asked you a question," the soldier barked. "What is your name?"

Closing her eyes for a second, Gabi tried to steady herself. She must remain calm and think carefully about what she would say. Glancing at Mr. Kos for reassurance, she answered, "My grandfather told you who I am. We're here to help him with the cows and with chores on the farm." She stood tall, unflinching as the soldier's eyes bore down on her. Inside, she was panic stricken.

The soldier stared at her for another moment, then nodded, and turned back to Mr. Kos. "Alright," he said. "You can go. But if you see anything suspicious, you must report it to us immediately. Do you understand?"

"Of course," replied Mr. Kos. "Children, move the cows toward home." Gabi, Max, and Eva moved past the soldiers toward the farmhouse. Max began to whistle softly to the cows to move them ahead. It looked as though they would soon be back in the safety of the barn.

"Just a moment. Stop!" The Nazi soldier called out again. Mr. Kos and the children froze and turned slowly to the soldier. He stared, first at Gabi, then at Eva, and finally at Max. "These two," he said, pointing to Gabi and Eva. "They look like they could be yours. But this one," he pointed directly at Max. "He looks different."

Once more Gabi felt the panic creep up on her. This nightmare was never going to end, she thought. Of course, the soldier was referring to her hair color and her eyes. She and Eva were both blond and blue-eyed. They both looked like locals. But Max was a different story. With his dark hair and dark eyes, he looked unusual, as though he didn't belong to this family. He looked like a Jew.

Max stared back at the soldier, without saying a word. Slowly, his hand moved toward the pocket of his jacket where his gun was hidden. Gabi gasped inside, fearing what her cousin might do. But before he could do anything, Mr. Kos spoke up once more.

"My grandchildren are all so different," he said, moving between the soldier and Max. "The girls look like their mother, but not the boy." With that, Mr. Kos took off his cap to reveal his full head of thick, dark hair. "The boy takes after his old grandfather, doesn't he?"

The soldier stared at Mr. Kos's head for a long moment and then looked back at Max. Finally, he turned and ordered his soldiers to move on, leaving Mr. Kos and the children standing in the field. For another moment, no one moved. Then Mr. Kos turned wearily to face Gabi, Max, and Eva. "Come, children," he said, weakly. "Move the cows back to the farmhouse and get inside."

Chapter Twenty-seven

SAFETY IN THE BARN

WORDLESSLY, Gabi, Max, and Eva walked back to the farm. They were still shaken and barely took notice of the cows that trailed on their own behind them. Nightmarish thoughts of their confrontation with the Nazi patrol swirled inside Gabi's head. What if the Nazis had questioned them further? What if they had discovered that Gabi and Max were Jewish? What would have happened to them and to Mr. Kos and Eva? Yet, somehow, none of those things had happened. Once more, they had eluded arrest.

Inside the barn, Gabi and Max fell into Mama's waiting arms. "Oh my children, my children," she wailed, swaying back and forth. They stood huddling together for several minutes, Mama silently giving thanks for the safe return of the children.

Finally, Mama pulled away and looked at the children. "I saw everything," she gasped. "I felt so helpless, watching from the barn. I saw the Nazis approaching and watched them surround you with their guns pointed at your heads. I wanted to run outside and throw myself in front of those guns. Oh my darlings, if anything had happened to you, I don't know what I would have done." Again, she pulled Gabi and Max close to her, squeezing them with fervor.

"Mama, I was so worried about you too," said Gabi, muffled against her mother's shoulder.

"We're fine, Auntie Judith," said Max, weakly. "I knew we were going to be alright." But Max sounded shaken and unsure of himself, trying to sound brave for the sake of his aunt. He could not believe how close he had come to being discovered and exposing all of them. Even as he had reached for the gun inside his jacket, he was not sure what he would have done with it.

Eva was watching the trio from a corner of the barn, wrapped protectively in the arms of her own grandfather. Both of them had tears in their eyes.

"Eva, thank you," said Gabi turning around, choking on her words. "If it weren't for you, we would have never made our way back to the pasture and to your grandfather."

Her grandfather looked at Eva and smiled. "I told you my Evichka knows her way around this forest."

Mama nodded strongly. "Yes, Eva," she said. "Thank you for leading my children back to me. You're a very brave girl."

"I was so scared back there with the Nazi soldiers," Eva admitted.

Gabi threw her arms around Eva's neck, squeezing her tightly. "Me too," she whispered. "I'm glad you're my friend."

"What about me?" said Max. "You're *my* friend too."

Eva smiled and nodded. "I'd never forget about you, Max."

"None of us will ever forget you, Max," continued Mr. Kos, smiling as he removed his own cap. "I guess I'm a lucky old man to have my full head of hair. And you're a lucky boy because of it."

Max grinned in return. "Maybe we're really related, Mr. Kos."

As they stood there, they realized that they had outwitted the Nazis by convincing them that Mr. Kos, a Catholic farmer, was related to Max, a Jewish boy. For a moment, no one spoke. And then slowly, Mama, Mr. Kos, Gabi, Eva, and Max all began to chuckle and then laugh out loud. The laugh felt good and satisfying.

Gabi and her family said goodnight to Mr. Kos and Eva and returned to their hiding place. Gabi fell onto the hay, drained of energy, unable to say another word. Max lay down next to her and, in a moment, he was asleep. Mama sat in a corner looking at her children. It would be some time before she could relax and sleep. For now, she just wanted to watch over Gabi and Max and pray for their ongoing safety.

Despite her exhaustion, Gabi had a hard time falling asleep. She could not forget the close encounter they had just had with the Nazi soldiers. She could not wipe out from her mind the dark, sinister eyes of the Nazi commander, staring at her with a look that pierced like steel knives.

Gabi dug through the hay for her porcelain doll. She had not held it for some time. In the preceding months, her life had been consumed with the partisans and her efforts to help them. She pulled the doll close, searching for something that reminded her of home. Somewhere inside of Gabi was a distant memory of a normal life, where she played in a park with her friends, went to school, and slept in a real bed. But at that moment, it was hard to imagine ever returning to that world. Gabi felt exhausted and old.

And then, in what felt like her darkest moment, Gabi began to think about her father. It had been some time since she had thought about him — his kind face and warm smile. But that face appeared in front of her now, as she tried to calm herself. "I am always here to protect you and keep you safe," Papa would say. "Sleep tight, Gabilinka." Gabi closed her eyes, praying that her father's words would hold true.

Chapter Twenty-eight

February 1945

OCCUPATION

A WEEK AFTER the children's encounter with the soldiers on the hillside field, the entire village was occupied by the Nazis. Troops were everywhere — on the roads, in the woods, in the church. They patrolled below the barn on a daily basis. Gabi and her family had to sit so quietly and so still, that Gabi's legs often cramped beneath her. Stretching at the end of the day was painful.

In retaliation for the partisan activities in the woods, the Nazis set fire to Olsavica's town hall. It was a warning to everyone in the village that defying Nazi command would result in terrible consequences. This time it was only a building that burned. Next time, it would be the villagers. And still the reports on the radio were hopeful. The Allies were liberating more concentration camps. And the Russians had entered eastern Germany, pushing the Nazis ever closer to defeat.

Gabi often thought of the partisans. She wondered where they were and what they were doing. She knew they would not be stopped — that they would continue to inflict as much damage to the Nazis as they could, even if it meant sacrificing themselves for their cause. She longed to be with them, scouting on their behalf, doing something productive.

But she knew that was impossible. The night of the ambush on the partisan camp was the last time the children went on a night walk. Even Max, for all his daring, never asked to go out again. For the next several months, Gabi, Max, and Mama stayed in the barn. They came into the house only for short periods of time and only when it was very dark. Mrs. Kos was more terrified than ever when they would appear in her kitchen. She fed them quickly and then pointed them back to their hiding place. Gabi couldn't even spend time with Eva anymore. It was just too dangerous to linger in the house.

These thoughts swirled in Gabi's head on a cold morning, months later. Mama was coming down with the flu. Her eyes were red, her nose was runny, and she was trying desperately to stifle the coughs that threatened to erupt and break the silence in the hayloft. Even a sneeze might give them away.

"Mama, I'm going to go inside the house," Gabi whispered, crawling over the hay to sit next to her mother. Mama lay huddled under all the blankets they had.

"No," Mama croaked. "Not during the day. It's too dangerous." She buried her face in the blanket to muffle the sound of a cough.

"Mama, you must have something hot to drink. I'll only be a minute. I promise."

Despite Mama's protests, Gabi moved the bundle of hay aside, nodded to Max, and crawled through the tunnel into the barn. Down the steps she moved, pausing periodically to listen for any sound that might be suspicious. But, so far, all was quiet.

Silently, she crept through the curtain and into the house. She could hear Mrs. Kos at work in the kitchen. Gabi moved swiftly past the bedroom and was just about to enter the kitchen, when suddenly she heard a knock at the front door. Gabi froze and dove back into the bedroom.

"Hello," a voice from outside called. "Maria, are you there?"

Unaware of Gabi's presence in the house, Mrs. Kos opened the door, welcoming her neighbor into her house.

"How are you, Olga?" said Mrs. Kos to her neighbor.

"Well, as fine as I can be with all those soldiers in the village. Still, it's probably better to have the Nazis here, than to worry about partisan hooligans running through the village. I can tell you this, if I hear anything about partisan activities, I'll report it to the Nazis in a second. I'm not going to take any risks at this point. It's just like reporting Jews. Better to turn them over to the Nazis than to have more trouble on our heads, right?"

"Well, um, I don't know, um, well, yes. Yes, Olga. Whatever you say." Mrs. Kos stammered. Luckily, her neighbor hardly seemed to notice.

"But from what I hear, the Nazis won't last long in our town," the neighbor continued. "Soon, it will be the Russians that are here. One army or another, in the long run it makes no difference to us, does it, Maria?"

"Yes … yes, of course," said Mrs. Kos. "Is there something I can get you, Olga?"

"I've just come to return the spool of thread I borrowed last week," the neighbor replied. "I used only a small amount."

The two women talked for a few minutes longer, while Gabi pressed herself against the wall, listening closely. She could hardly believe what she was hearing. Was it possible that the Russian army was so close?

Mrs. Kos and her neighbor finished their conversation and Gabi heard the door close. She waited a minute longer and then walked quietly down the hallway, into the kitchen, pausing momentarily to savor the warmth coming from the stove. Mrs. Kos was standing at the kitchen sink with her back to Gabi, washing some dishes. Gabi glanced around and cleared her throat.

"Excuse me, Mrs. Kos," she said in a low voice.

Mrs. Kos spun around abruptly, sending a spray of water across the kitchen floor. "What do you want? What are you doing in here?" Mrs. Kos was panicked.

"I'm sorry, Mrs. Kos," Gabi began. "Mama is —"

"We told you never to come out during the day. Why can't you listen to us? Are you trying to get us all killed?" Every muscle in Mrs. Kos's body spelled fear.

"Please, Mrs. Kos, Mama is sick. I need some tea for her. Please, just give me something hot for her to drink and I'll leave right away." Gabi moved forward to try and calm Mrs. Kos.

"My neighbor could return any moment," hissed Mrs. Kos, glancing anxiously at the front door. "Didn't you hear what she said about reporting Jews? She'll report us as well."

Gabi stared at Mrs. Kos who stood trembling and twisting her apron into a knot, sweat beading on her forehead. She felt sorry for this poor woman. Mr. Kos had said his wife was a good person who knew in her heart that she was doing the right thing by hiding Gabi's family. At the moment, Mrs. Kos looked like a cornered animal with terror in her eyes. Gabi pitied her, having to live each day with such fear. Still, Gabi would not leave the kitchen without something for Mama.

"It will only take a moment. I'll help you make the tea and then I'll leave."

"I don't want your help. I don't need your help. Haven't we done everything we can for you? Why do you insist on trying to get us into trouble? Just stay in the barn. Just stay out of my sight." Mrs. Kos continued to pace anxiously, looking out the window for any sign of her neighbor. Gabi didn't budge.

"Fine," said Mrs. Kos, reluctantly. "I'll make your tea and then, please, you must go back to the barn."

Gabi nodded. Mrs. Kos quickly prepared some hot tea in a large cup. "Give this to your mother as well," she said, pushing a bottle of liquid medicine into Gabi's hands. "It will help her sleep. Now please," she pleaded desperately, "go!"

Gabi thanked Mrs. Kos and then walked swiftly out of the kitchen and into the barn. Up the ladder she moved, balancing the tea and the medicine in one hand. She pushed aside the bundle of hay and crawled through the tunnel into their hiding space.

"Gabi," whispered Mama, weakly, "I was worried. What took you so long?"

"It was nothing, Mama," Gabi replied. "Mrs. Kos was looking for some medicine for you. Here, take some. She said it would make you feel better."

Mama poured some of the liquid into her mouth and sipped her tea. "Thank you, Gabilinka. I'm glad you're here to help take care of me." She settled back into the hay, while Gabi crawled over to another corner. She could not bring herself to tell Mama the news she had heard from the kitchen. Mama needed her rest right now. Gabi didn't want to excite her or disappoint her, if the news wasn't true. It was too wonderful to believe that the Russians were close by, that they might be moving toward this village. Gabi decided to keep the news to herself for now.

Chapter Twenty-nine

May 1945

LIBERATION

IT SEEMED LIKE an ordinary warm spring day in May 1945. Like every other day, Gabi rolled over in the hay, opening her eyes and stretching carefully. Other than using the toilet pail once a day, they had not been allowed out of their hiding place since Gabi had gone into the kitchen to get tea for Mama. Mr. Kos explained apologetically that his wife was becoming more agitated about having them in the house. It would be better if they just stayed in the barn, he said. So, from that day on, Mr. Kos brought them their food to the hayloft at night.

Gabi slowly moved her sore legs from side to side, back and forth. Next to her, Max and Mama were doing the same thing. Gabi called it their morning exercise. And while the three of them shifted and extended their arms and legs, they listened for sounds from outside. Usually they heard soldiers moving past the barn or farmers taking their cattle to the hills. On this morning, there was suddenly a peculiar sound, the sound of someone shouting from inside the house.

"What is that?" asked Gabi, sitting up suddenly. Even her back and neck were stiff from lack of movement.

The shouts continued, growing with intensity, closer and closer. For a moment Gabi, Max, and Mama froze. Was it a warning that danger was approaching? Were the Nazis coming to search the barn? Had Gabi and her family finally been discovered? But these sounds were different. It wasn't the sound of danger. It was the sound of laughter and joy.

"Gabi, Max, get up! You won't believe what's happened. Get up!" The voice came nearer and nearer.

"It's Eva," cried Gabi. "Move the bale of hay. Let her in."

Quickly, Max shoved the stack of hay aside, as Eva tumbled through the tunnel into their hiding space.

"Gabi, you've got to come outside. You've got to see this."

"Eva, slow down. What is it? What's happening?" Gabi grabbed onto Eva, urging her to calm down and make some sense.

"The Nazis have gone. They've left. We woke up this morning and they had disappeared, just like that."

Gabi could not quite comprehend the news. "But what does it mean that they're gone? Is there another troop coming to take their place? I don't understand." Desperately she turned to her mother and Max who looked equally confused.

"No," said Eva, shaking her head. "I didn't tell you the best part. The Russian troops are coming. We can see the tanks in the distance. It's on the radio. Germany has surrendered. The Nazis have been defeated!" Eva screamed this last piece of news into Gabi's face and then fell back, laughing uncontrollably.

Gabi sat back on her heels in stunned silence. Then she turned once more to face her family. "Mama, can it be true?" she asked. Mama shook her head in disbelief.

"What are we waiting for?" said Max. "I'm going outside." And with that, Max dove for the tunnel, barreling through with an energy he had not shown for months. Only a moment passed before Gabi flew after him, with Mama close behind, their aches and pains forgotten in that moment. They dashed down the ladder and ran through the curtain into the house, where Mr. Kos sat listening to the radio. Mrs. Kos hovered nearby, pacing.

"It's true, Judith," Mr. Kos said, looking up and seeing the expression on their faces. "The reports say that Adolf Hitler has committed suicide to avoid arrest. All across Europe, his armies are surrendering to the Allies. It's over. The nightmare is over." With that, Mr. Kos lowered his head onto the table and wept. Mama moved over and placed her hand on his shoulder.

"We have to go outside," said Eva, tugging on Gabi's arm. "Listen! The Russian soldiers are coming. There are people cheering in the road. It's a celebration."

"Can we go?" asked Max. It was unbelievable that they were actually allowed to go outside.

Mama nodded and turned to Stephan. "Come outside, Stephan," she said. "You deserve to be part of the celebration." He looked up, wiping the tears from his eyes.

All of them went out to the village road. It was so strange for Gabi to be walking out the front door of the Kos farmhouse. The last time she had used this door was sixteen months earlier when they had first arrived. Then, she felt she was walking toward a great fearful unknown. Now she was walking toward freedom. The air outside was clean and warm. Gabi closed her eyes and filled her lungs with its freshness. She could smell spring and it made her dizzy.

"Gabi, look," cried Max. "Look at the Russian tanks."

Sure enough, the Russian army was approaching and moving through the town. Villagers lined the road, cheering and throwing flowers at the soldiers who waved and smiled in return. Gabi screamed and waved her arms. Max shouted next to her, whistling and stamping his feet. Eva jumped up and down and called out to the soldiers. Mama stood quietly with Mr. Kos, tears rolling down both their cheeks.

Behind the Russian soldiers, Gabi caught sight of her partisan friends, lead by Vladimir, the rebel leader, marching triumphantly. She called out to Vladimir who waved in reply.

"Ah, it's my young scouts. It's good to see you again. It's good to see all of us alive." He grinned and gave Gabi and Max a victory sign.

Max searched the crowd for Dominik, but he couldn't see him anywhere. He felt disappointed, but shrugged it away. Nothing was going to spoil this moment.

The celebration continued for hours. People sang and danced in the streets. Strangers hugged and twirled each other on the road. And finally, near the end of the day, Gabi turned to Mama and fell into her arms.

The two of them pulled Max into their embrace. There they stood, hugging tightly, clutching each other with intense love and relief. Finally, Gabi pulled away and looked deeply into her mother's eyes. Their glance said it all. They had survived. They were alive. And now, they would be going home.

Chapter Thirty

FRIENDSHIP

IT TOOK SEVERAL MORE WEEKS to organize their transportation back home. While they waited for Joseph to arrive with the truck, Gabi spent the days walking in the fresh air. After being imprisoned indoors for so many months, she wanted to spend as much time in the outdoors as she possibly could. These days, her walks through the forest took place during the day. Now she could walk slowly, savoring each step, admiring the beauty of the mountains in the springtime.

On their very last day in the mountain village, Max joined Gabi on a walk into the woods. Without even thinking, their path led them close to the road that they had watched with Eva on their night walks, the road the Nazis had fought to complete for their last stand. How ironic that this very road was the one used by the Russian army to claim victory over the Nazis.

As they stood by the road, lost in their own thoughts, there was a sudden rustling in the leaves behind them. Gabi and Max whirled around, almost expecting Nazi soldiers. It was still hard to shake the need to hide. But on this warm day in May, it was not Nazi soldiers who emerged from the forest to greet Gabi and Max.

"I'm sorry. I didn't mean to startle you." Dominik pushed the branches of a tree aside, stepped over a downed log, and joined Gabi and Max on the hill overlooking the road.

"We didn't see you during the parade through the village," Max said. He was relieved to see that Dominik was safe. "I looked everywhere for you."

"I was back at the campsite, closing it down and collecting some gear. That's why I came looking for you, today." He glanced warmly at Gabi and Max. "I guess you'll be going back home now."

"I'm going back to Gabi's home," said Max, sadly looking down at the ground. Joseph had arrived the night before with heartbreaking news about Max's family. The transport that had taken his parents and sister away had headed straight for Auschwitz. Max's family had been killed, along with hundreds of thousands of Jewish prisoners. Max was returning home to live with Gabi and her mother. From now on, he really would be Gabi's brother.

Dominik nodded with understanding, as Max explained. "Your parents would be proud of you, Max. I'm sure of it. And you're lucky you've got family to live with." Dominik reached out to put his arm on Max's shoulder. Max sniffled, wiped his nose, and nodded.

"And what about you?" asked Gabi. "Where are you going?"

Dominik shrugged. "I'm staying with Vladimir. There's still so much to do, rounding up Nazis who might now be hiding in the forest. I guess I'm not finished being a soldier yet."

Max looked up at Dominik, once again admiring his strength and courage. Dominik had given Max such hope at a time when he had felt so hopeless. Max reached into his back pocket and pulled out his gun. Then he took a deep breath. "I want you to have this," he said, holding it out to Dominik.

"But that's yours, Max," said Dominik. "I fixed it for you."

Max shook his head. "No, I don't think I want to be a soldier anymore. You might need it more than me."

Dominik took the gun and reached out to shake Max's hand. "You were a great soldier, Max. Never forget that." Then he turned to Gabi. "You were a great soldier too. I'm glad I met you."

Gabi stared at the hand that Dominik held out for her to shake. Then, she pushed it aside, reached over, and hugged him warmly. Their lives had come together at such an important time. Yet she knew that it was unlikely she would see him again. "Good luck, Dominik," she whispered. Then she turned back to Max.

"Come on," said Gabi, gently. "We don't want to miss our ride home." The two young people took one last look at Dominik, then turned and walked out of the woods and back to the farmhouse.

Mama stood outside, saying good-by to Mr. and Mrs. Kos. "I know how difficult this has been for you," Mama said, looking directly at Mrs. Kos. "But please know that we are grateful to you for everything." Mama reached forward and grasped Mrs. Kos's hands.

Still Mrs. Kos could not look into Mama's eyes. Her head darted nervously as she said, "We did the right thing by having you here. I … I never would have turned you in. You know that. I … I'm glad you're safe." It was the warmest statement that Mrs. Kos had spoken in the year and a half that Gabi and her family had been there.

Mama nodded with understanding as she shook Mrs. Kos's hands. "I know you are a good person," Mama said. Mrs. Kos managed a quick squeeze and then headed for the farmhouse, hands still wringing in despair. Then, Mr. Kos came forward to shake Mama's hands.

"Thank you, Stephan," said Mama. "Thank you for everything. We owe our lives to you." Mr. Kos nodded and lowered his eyes. He could not bring himself to speak.

Father Lensky was there to see Gabi's family off. He shook hands with each of them, wishing them well on their journey back home.

Finally, Gabi was left standing with Eva. Eva eyed Gabi curiously with her sharp blue eyes. It was that same inquisitive look that months earlier Gabi had found so uncomfortable. But now it was no longer intimidating.

"You must be glad to be leaving this place," said Eva.

Gabi paused. "I'm glad we don't have to hide anymore. But I'll miss you, Eva."

Eva's face brightened. "Will you?"

"Of course I will. You're my friend." Gabi spoke truthfully. "And besides, how could I ever forget what we've been through together."

"Will I ever see you again?" asked Eva.

"I hope so," Gabi replied.

Eva nodded. Who knew what would happen in the months and years to come. "Well, in case I don't, I want you to have this. Don't open it until you're on your way." Eva pushed an envelope into Gabi's hands, and then threw her arms around Gabi's neck. Gabi returned the hug, warmly. Then Eva turned to Max.

"Don't get into any more trouble, Max," she said, ruffling his hair. Max smiled and nodded.

Joseph stood watching and waiting, holding open the door to the truck. Gabi looked toward the truck unhappily. She didn't want to sit in any more cramped places.

"Gabi," said Joseph, as if reading her mind. "Will you sit up front with me? We can keep the windows open as wide as you like."

Gabi smiled at Joseph and her mother. "I'd love that, Joseph." They all piled into Joseph's truck for the journey back home.

It was only when they were out of sight of the Kos farm and the village that Gabi finally looked down at the envelope in her hands. She turned it over once or twice and then opened it. Gabi stared down at the picture that fell out of the envelope. It was the photo Eva had taken of Gabi during their first week in hiding. The young girl stared back at her — terrified but strong — from the black and white picture. Gabi flipped the photo over and read the words that Eva had written on the back: "A souvenir for my friend."

Epilogue

May 1997

In 1997, I traveled to the former Czechoslovakia to visit the town where my mother, Gabi, had grown up. I also traveled to the mountain village of Olsavica. As I stood on a hill overlooking the grassy farmlands of eastern Slovakia, the sun shone brightly on a warm spring day. I wondered if it had been this beautiful that day in May 1945, when the town had been liberated by the Russian army.

For me, it had been a long journey getting here. More than fifty years had passed since my mother had hidden in the hayloft in one of these barns. I had heard my mother's stories from the time I was a young girl. They were daring stories — scary at times, but also bold and exciting. They had become my favorite bedtime stories. I was overcome with longing to visit the village, to look up at the mountains surrounding the town and to see the farmhouse. I vowed that one day I would come to this country and to this village, to see for myself where my mother's adventure had taken place. And finally, now a mother of my own children, I was here.

Eva Kos was expecting me. As I approached the village,

I wondered what it was going to be like to meet the real Eva, now an old woman. In my mother's stories, Eva had at first seemed so suspicious and untrustworthy. Eva and I had corresponded by mail for many months, while the plans were being made for my visit to the village.

As I approached the house at the end of the road, I smiled. It was just as my mother had described it — the fourth last house from the end of the road, on the left side — a small white house with a red gate. The only thing missing was the red scarf tied to the gate. I got out of my rented car and approached the gate. I opened it, and walked into the yard, glancing over to look at the barn to one side of the house. There it was, attached to the house, just as my mother had described. My heart began to beat faster as I glanced up at one corner of the barn. That's where their hiding place was, I thought.

Suddenly, in front of me, the door opened and a small elderly woman emerged. She had short, cropped hair, graying in places, and lovely sparkling blue eyes.

"You're Eva?" I asked. My Slovak was weak, but passable.

Eva nodded. "And you must be Gabi's daughter." I caught my breath at the mention of my mother's name. "I'm so glad to finally meet you," she said. "When you wrote and told me that Gabi had died, I was so sad. But when you said you wanted to come and visit, it brought me such happiness. Even if I didn't get to see your mother again after the war ended, I'm so glad that you are here now."

I paused, swallowing back my own tears. It had only

been six months since my mother had died and the memory was still very painful. "My mother … Gabi … always wanted to come and see you," I managed to say. "She talked about it all the time, especially after her own mother, my grandmother, had died. But she never had the chance."

Eva nodded. "We knew it would be hard to see each other after Gabi returned to her own village. And then, when she left Czechoslovakia for North America, I knew it would be impossible. Our lives were meant to go in different directions."

"It was too hard for my family to remain in this country after the war ended," I continued, almost apologetically. "Once they had returned to their village, they realized that there were too many sad memories there. They had lost too many friends and family members."

"Yes," said Eva. "My grandfather always said that the world went mad during that time." Eva pointed back to the farmhouse. "After they died, my grandparents left me their farm. They knew how much I loved this place, this land, and these forests. I've lived here ever since." Eva paused again, then asked cautiously. "And Max?"

"He's well. He sends his fondest regards. He's told me that he was quite difficult when he was hiding here. Is that true?"

Eva smiled and nodded. "Yes, he was full of life. But Gabi and I were just as unruly. We caused great anxiety for your grandmother and for my grandparents."

Eva and I stood there a moment, both lost in their own memories. I was the first to break the silence. "Eva," I said.

"I have something to show you." I reached into my pocket and withdrew a single black and white photograph. It was slightly tattered at the edges and had been looked at so often that it was crinkled and worn. I ran my hands over the photo, smoothing out the creases. When I handed it to Eva, she gasped with pleasure. After a moment, she turned the photo over and smiled in recognition at her own inscription on the back: "A souvenir for my friend."

"I can't believe she kept it all these years," whispered Eva. "Look how young she was — how young all of us were."

"Will you tell me the stories?" I asked. "Will you tell me about the night walks, about spying for the partisans? My mother told me often about them. I want to hear the stories from you, as well."

Eva smiled ever so slightly. "Oh, there is so much to tell, so much you should know. Come inside," she said. "We'll have tea and we can begin to talk. I'll tell you the stories and you can tell me about Gabi's life after the war."

I nodded and followed Eva as she turned to enter the farmhouse. She clutched the photograph as if it was the key transporting her back to another time. At the door, Eva paused, looked down at the picture again, and then turned to face me.

"By the way," Eva said. "You look just like Gabi."

I smiled. It was the greatest compliment I could receive.

Author's Note

THE STORY

WHILE MANY OF the characters in *The Night Spies* are fictional, the story is inspired by the true experiences of my family in Czechoslovakia in the years 1944 to 1945. My mother's name was Gabi. The real Gabi lived with her mother and younger brother. Their father had died before World War II began. Once the war began, as Jews Gabi and her family lived in constant fear of being arrested and sent to a concentration camp. These camps were prison compounds where millions of Jews were detained, tortured, and killed over the course of World War II. In 1942, Gabi was forced to hide in a dresser in her mother's dining room, while Nazi soldiers searched through the house looking for her.

By the beginning of 1944, Gabi and her family knew they could no longer safely remain in their house. They made plans to leave their home and go into hiding in a small mountain village called Olsavica in the northern part of Czechoslovakia. They believed they would be safer in this tiny village, where the priest was sympathetic to Jews and willing to offer assistance. Here, they hid until the war ended in May 1945.

In my story, Gabi and her family stay with one Catholic farmer. In reality, they had to change locations several times, moving to other farmhouses whenever there was a threat that Nazi soldiers might search the village. These farmers and their families risked their own lives to help Gabi and other Jewish families. Eva is a fictional character created from my own encounter with a young girl named Evichka, when I visited Slovakia in 1997.

In the forest surrounding Olsavica, there really was a partisan troop. It is also true that the Nazis were building a road for defense that ran close to the village. While it was dangerous to leave their hiding place and go into the forest, Gabi's brother and several other young people served as scouts for the partisans, alerting them if Nazis were approaching.

THE HISTORY

WORLD WAR II BEGAN on September 1, 1939, when Germany invaded Poland. Adolf Hitler, leader of the Nazi party that ruled Germany, sent his army through Europe, intent on crushing anyone who got in their way. It was Hitler's goal to rule Europe and rid the world of all Jews, who he believed were responsible for many of Germany's economic problems. Collaborating with Hitler, countries like Italy, Hungary, and Romania formed what was known as the Axis Powers. The Allied Powers, which included countries such as Canada, the United States, Great Britain, and the

Soviet Union, opposed the Axis.

In 1938, before the start of World War II, Hitler's army had already occupied the western part of Czechoslovakia, known as Sudetenland. The eastern part of Czechoslovakia, known as Slovakia, declared its independence and was run by the Hlinka Slovak People's Party, a pro-Nazi army that collaborated with Adolf Hitler and governed on his behalf. By 1939, Slovakia had signed a Treaty of Protection with Nazi Germany and the Nazis began sending troops into Slovakia.

Throughout all of Czechoslovakia, the conditions for Jews were dangerous and life threatening. At first, rules were put in place to restrict their freedom. Soon, Jews were arrested and deported to concentration camps by the thousands. There, they were put to work, starved, tortured, and killed.

During this time, it was against the law for any citizen to help a Jew. Any person who was caught hiding Jews could be imprisoned or killed. In spite of these dangers, there were some honorable people who offered assistance to Jewish families — feeding them, helping them escape, and hiding them in safe places. These righteous people bravely risked their own lives and the lives of their families to resist the enemy.

Hiding in the mountains and forests of Czechoslovakia and other countries, there were other groups of people who fought the Nazis with weapons. Known as partisans, they banded together in small rebel groups, using guerrilla tactics. They bombed Nazi installations, smuggled arms and ammunition, disrupted enemy communications, and generally interfered with the progress of the Nazis.

In August 1944, partisan groups throughout Slovakia launched a large-scale assault on their Nazi occupiers. This became known as the Slovak National Uprising. The assault began in a town called Banska Bystrica. In a coordinated effort, partisan units in other parts of the country continued the battle, setting fire to Nazi factories and blowing up Nazi machinery. Though the partisans suffered heavy losses, their uprising helped disrupt the Nazis, after which Allied troops closed in.

In May 1945, the Allies defeated Germany. Russian troops liberated Slovakia, while other Allied armies liberated other countries across Europe. But by the time Nazi Germany was defeated, six million Jewish people had been killed across Europe.

The Night Spies is based on this history and on my family's story. And while we can never begin to fully imagine how much they suffered during this tragic time in history, I am always gratefully aware of the fact that my family members were among the lucky ones. They survived to tell their stories and to pass them on to me, as I pass them on to you.

WORLD WAR II AND CZECHOSLOVAKIA

—

January 1933

Adolf Hitler is appointed Chancellor of Germany.

September 1938

The Munich Conference. Great Britain, Italy, and France sign a pact with Germany, agreeing to the German occupation of the western part of Czechoslovakia (known as Sudetenland).

October 1938

Nazi troops occupy the Sudetenland.

November 1938

Kristallnacht (night of broken glass). Anti-Jewish attacks in Germany, Austria, and the Sudetenland. Two hundred synagogues are destroyed; 7,500 Jewish shops are looted; 30,000 Jews are sent to concentration camps.

March 1939

Italy, Hungary, and Romania become part of the Axis Powers. The eastern part of Czechoslovakia (known as Slovakia) signs a Treaty of Protection with Nazi Germany. Hitler sends in troops for Slovakia's "protection."

June 1939

Slovakia passes its own version of the Nuremberg Laws, a series of rules that restrict the freedom of Jews. Jewish workers and managers are dismissed from jobs. Jewish businesses are taken over by non-Jewish individuals. Jewish children are not allowed to go to non-Jewish schools. Jews are required to wear a yellow star of David on every article of clothing in order to identify them publicly as Jews. Bicycles, radios, and personal luxury items must be turned over to the Nazis. Over the next few years, restrictions against Jews continue to increase.

Yad Vashem Archive

Members of the Hlinka guard march in Slovakia.

September 1939

Hitler invades Poland, marking the beginning of World War II. England and France declare war on Germany.

October 1939

The first Slovak Jews are deported to concentration camps in Poland. By October 1942, 75 percent of Slovak Jews have been deported.

May 1940

Auschwitz concentration camp is opened in Poland.

November 1941

Theresienstadt concentration camp is established near Prague, Czechoslovakia. Nazis use it for propaganda purposes.

December 1941

Hitler declares war on the United States. The United States declares war on Germany.

1942-1944

The Jews of Slovakia continue to be deported to concentration camps. The government of Slovakia pays Germany for every deported Jew. Of the 137,000 Jews in pre-war Slovakia, more than 72,000 die in concentration camps.

August 1944

Slovak National Uprising. Partisan groups throughout Slovakia launch a large-scale assault on their Nazi occupiers. The partisans attempt to hold out against the Nazis until the Russians arrive. Over the course of several months, they use every opportunity to attack the Nazis and, in turn, suffer heavy losses. However, their missions help to disrupt the Nazis as the Allied troops close in.

A group of partisan men and women on a march.

June 1944

D-Day. Allied landings in Normandy, France.

April 1945

Adolf Hitler commits suicide in his bunker in Berlin, Germany.

May 1945

Unconditional German surrender. Russian troops liberate Czechoslovakia.

The real Gabi and her brother, in happier times before the war.

Gabi (right) and her mother (below) in 1944. These photos were taken outside the barn in the small mountain village of Olsavica, where they hid during the war. They are dressed in peasant clothing borrowed from the villagers.

After the war, an older Gabi stands in front of Hrad Castle, near her hometown of Granč, in what is now Slovakia.

Below: Hrad Castle and Granč today.

The mountain village of Olsavica — where Gabi and her family hid nearly 60 years ago — as it is today.

The author, Kathy Kacer, with Stephan Blasčak, the real "Joseph," who helped Gabi (Kathy's mother) and her family escape to Olsavica (left).

The Suhy family (Mr. and Mrs. Suhy and their granddaughter, Evichka), at right. The Kos family was based upon them.

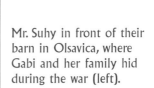

Mr. Suhy in front of their barn in Olsavica, where Gabi and her family hid during the war (left).